SINFUL LOVE

SINFUL LOVE

SANJANA NIDHI

To all the girls out there who love fiercely.

CHAPTER 1

Rochelle

"Have a good one." I smile at one of our regulars as I place the soy latte on the counter. It is around noon time now. Usually, Jake helps me out as the crowd at this time of the day doubles in number, but I'm all alone today in the café.

I'm heating a jug to prepare the next order when a lady cuts the line and slams her hand on the counter. I jump a little, startled by the loud bang.

"Where's my order? I've been standing here for the last ten minutes."

"I apologize for the delay, but I have to serve the ones before you, ma'am." I offer her an apologetic smile. I try to calm my breathing as I set to make two flat whites.

I wrote her order on the cup only a minute ago, and she's aware that there are two more customers due before her.

I'm closing the lid of the cup when she starts again. "Do you think I have all day to waste? Hurry the hell up!" she grits out.

The people waiting in queue stare in my direction when she starts raising her voice.

Swallowing the lump that forms in my throat, I try to placate her with a polite smile. "I'm sorry. I'm on it."

I prepare her iced tea with blistering speed. Maybe I should give her a muffin coupon.

I'm not allowed to give them away as they're reserved for special occasions, but I could pay for one. She must be having a bad day, and this is the least I could do.

Before handing her the iced tea, I walk the small distance to the coupons drawer and take one out.

"That's it! I'm outta here." She exclaims and I jerk around.

"Please, wait! Here's your drink." I hurry to the counter with her cup in hand but trip over my own feet.

I don't fall but my abdomen crashes against the counter, making me wince.

"You stupid bitch!" I look up and am horrified to see the woman's shirt covered in iced tea.

I glance at my hand and feel the color drain from my face when I see the lid missing from the cup.

I must've forgotten to put the lid on. And now, it's half-empty.

Grabbing the box of tissues, I round the counter.

"I'm so sorry." I take a few tissues and reach for her blouse to dab at it, but she pushes my hand away.

"Don't touch me! Where's your manager?!" she snarls, and I feel my eyes sting.

"M-ma'am, I'm sorry, please, let me h-help you." I try to approach her again to offer her the tissues, but she shouts and pushes me hard on the chest.

The breath is knocked out of my lungs and I stagger back, immediately losing my balance.

I start to fall backward and screw my eyes shut in fear.

A strong arm encircles my waist, and I am suspended mid-fall.

I open my eyes slowly and am instantly trapped in the strangely deep and inquiring dark brown eyes.

He straightens with me, his hand still clutching my waist.

That's when I notice his height. He is a foot taller than me.

With a free hand, he reaches my face and wipes under my eyes. His gesture makes me realize I'm crying.

"You're okay." He says in that clear, low timbre that makes me shiver.

He isn't asking me. He's telling me that I'm okay.

And somehow, I believe him.

My erratic heartbeats return to normal. Maybe it was the soft British accent that calmed me down because everything else fades away.

I take deep breaths and his hand—that's still around my waist—slides up and down in slow movements, encouraging me, appraising me.

The gesture oddly relaxes me further.

Not once did he break eye contact.

When he is certain, only then he lets go of me, albeit hesitantly. Like his hands don't want to part from me.

Suddenly, I become aware of my surroundings. I'm in the café. I just spilled a drink on one of the customers.

I look for her, but the man who was embracing me a minute ago is standing with his back to me, obstructing my view.

He speaks to someone in a low voice and I can't quite make out what he is saying.

I reach out a hand to get his attention but stop before my finger could connect his dark sweater.

He's so broad. I remember how he held me in his arms. No man has ever touched me like that in my entire life of eighteen years.

Or more like I never allowed it. My cheeks heat. It's a foreign feeling. A slight flutter inside of my chest. A little dip in my stomach.

I don't know what's happening to me.

After what feels like forever—when only a few minutes have passed—the mysterious man with chocolate eyes turns to face me.

I suck in a much-needed breath when I get a clearer view of him.

My savior is devastatingly beautiful. I take in his symmetrical features.

I've never seen a good-looking man like him before.

His jet-black hair is styled impeccably. There's not a single hair out of place.

His eyebrows are thick and black, like his hair.

Then there are those searching eyes of his which are roving over me as if he's trying to read me.

His perfectly sculpted nose gives him a striking look. He's cleanly shaven, which accentuates his sharp jaw and beautifully carved lips.

In my entire teen life, I have never known what it's like to have a crush on someone.

The few girls I used to be friends with at school often thought of me as a weird girl because I never took part in boys' talk.

Of course, they never said anything to my face. Who does that? But it was apparent in their hardly concealed grimace whenever they saw me coming.

The reason behind it was that I didn't have interesting things to chat about "boys".

And that's because I never dated.

It's not like my parents are strict. I've never dated by choice.

I choose to call myself an old-school kind of soul.

SINFUL LOVE

I know what nowadays romantic relationships are like. And I don't want that. I need someone who could tug at my heartstrings in the very first eye contact.

Never thought it could happen. Up until now. Is this it?

Is this mystery man my first ever crush?

"I'd like an espresso, please." He speaks.

My classmates often swooned over British accent, and I never got the hype. That was before. Now, hearing him speak in that elegant accent is doing unimaginable things to me.

"Miss?"

I blink twice to shake myself out of my stupor.

"Yes. Sorry. I'll get you a flat white right away." I murmur as I start to turn.

"Espresso." He corrects with a hint of amusement in his tone.

"Right. Yes." I squeak, flushing with embarrassment.

I quickly round the counter and get to work.

I take in the liquid mess on the counter which reminds me of the lady. I lift my head to search for her but find him instead.

"Don't worry about her." My savior says.

"B-but," With the slightest shake of his head, he halts my words.

I jerk a nod and swiftly write his order on the empty paper cup.

I feel his eyes as I bend to get the rag. Feel him watching me wipe the counter.

My fingers reach up to tuck the errant strands—that managed to escape my ponytail—behind my ear. I feel him track the movements of my hand.

A shiver takes over me. I repress it and resume making drinks.

He just stands at the side, taking me in when I hand out a cup to a customer.

My fingers fumble while writing another customer's order. The consciousness of being under his scrutiny is making me shy and nervous.

"Hey, Rochelle are you okay?" Lucinda, one of our regulars looks at me with concern. She is in her mid-forties and a teacher.

I give her a strained nod, reliving what just happened.

I am still in shock at how violently that woman behaved with me.

"God bless that man who saved you. I was at the end of the queue and before I could reach you, he was suddenly there."

My heart does a backflip at the mention of my savior.

"I don't know what he said to that rude lady because I barely saw his lips moving. But whatever he did, he managed to make her scarce in no time."

My movements halt. A spark of little something ignites my still out-of-control heart.

And although what happened to me was frightening, my mind is obsessing over the fact that the stranger stood up for me.

Lucinda misjudges my reaction to panic because she immediately launches into one of the stories of her students.

I laugh softly when she tells me about her student giving a hilarious excuse for arriving late to class.

The entire time I chat with her, my eyes want to look at him, but I refrain.

When it becomes unbearable, I decide to sneak a tiny peek at him.

My breathing quickens, and with a great deal of courage, I peer at him from beneath my lashes.

A small gasp escapes my lips when I find him looking straight at me.

I don't know what gets into me, but I don't look away. I don't want to. I have never felt a pull like this. Like my eyes are drawn to him.

I openly admire him. He is a sight to behold. I also notice that he's definitely older. Maybe in the mid-twenties.

This is the gutsiest thing I have done. I have never locked eyes with a boy before, much less a man.

And here I am, staring at a man who's older than me as if my eyes are starved. Starved for the sight of him.

I take my eyes off his reluctantly and fill his cup.

I purposely move slower. It feels like this is it. It's like I am going to lose him after he walks out of here.

What should I do? I am terrible at such things. I don't know how to flirt.

I feel every sort of helpless as I call out his order and he steps forward.

His fingers brush slightly against mine and I swear it's like I am the female main character in a romance novel.

I feel tingles inside of my chest. I also feel a bittersweet ache.

The sudden turmoil of feelings has me perplexed.

I don't say my usual 'have a nice day' or any other things I say to the customers when I hand them their order.

This oddly feels like a goodbye when in reality he is a total stranger.

He is silent too as he takes a step back. Then another. Then one more, all the while staring at me.

And then he finally turns to leave. I watch his back as he walks away.

I feel inexplicably empty.

My fingers reach for the silver heart bracelet around my left wrist to fiddle with—a habit I developed when I was only fourteen.

The bracelet was given by my late grandma. That woman was so courageous and headstrong, she was my rock.

Even years after her passing, one touch of my bracelet fills me with strength and a sense of contentment. With one graze, I feel closer to her.

But my fingers can't find it.

Frowning, I look down. My bracelet is missing.

My heart sinks and I start looking for it.

That day, I search every corner of the café for my bracelet. And when I still don't find it, a wry smile curls my lips.

Looks like the bracelet isn't the only thing I lost today.

CHAPTER 2

Rochelle

"Emily!" I cry out as I approach the open kitchen with hasty steps.

I seize the ceramic water jug from her grasp before she could pour more and make matters worse.

Manhandling her to the side, I take her place behind the kitchen counter and inspect the bowl.

My cinnamon rolls dough is ruined.

I love my big sister more than anything in this world, but today, her behavior is quite peculiar.

She is six years older than me but a child at heart.

Her unusual behavior and loud laughter are the things that make everyone adore her.

But today, she's not being her cute and funny self.

No. Since morning, she is fidgety and distracted.

She is a big-time foodie and I loved doing experiments in the kitchen, trying varieties of recipes. She had always enthusiastically volunteered in tasting it every time, announcing me as the "best cook in the whole wide world".

I tried convincing her to learn cooking but she was never interested.

Once, when she did try, she almost burned the house down. Since that incident, Emily swore off cooking completely.

Imagine my shock when she asked me for a cooking lesson this morning.

I had agreed but only after collecting my jaw from the floor.

I sensed her restlessness but didn't know the reason behind it.

So instead of probing her, I welcomed her to my zone—the kitchen.

Throughout the time I was explaining her the basics of cooking, she had a lost look on her face.

Last night, she skipped ranting about her British boss, Asher.

And that was unusual as hell because she does that religiously.

Which meant something had happened between them.

She works for a well-known Tech company called T&A.

Currently, she has started working from Asher's home as the bossman prefers it. And he specifically wanted Emily as his PA.

This ensued a cold war between them. But never once was Emily this quiet.

I patiently helped her make breakfast. But Emily in her absent-mindedness sprinkled powdered sugar in the omelet instead of salt.

And now she made the flour all runny by pouring more water than required.

I can handle anything but ruining food is not one of them!

"What?" She snaps.

"Look!" I point at the bowl.

I don't remember the last time I've raised my voice like this.

It can be because I've been tangled with my own issues from yesterday.

It's been twenty hours since my enigmatic savior walked out of the café without a second glance.

It's so ironic that my sister and I are all worked up over British men.

Ugh! Why are you so hung up over a total stranger, Rochelle? I reprimand myself internally. This is so unlike me.

But I feel connected to him. My heart murmurs.

I pinch the bridge of my nose as I feel a headache coming.

"I'm sorry!" Only my sister could apologize so violently.

I lower my hand and watch her green eyes that are a mirror image of mine, take in the mess.

I can't stand still any longer and watch her suffer like this. "That's it. Spill."

"What are you talking about?" she averts her eyes and heads to the living room.

Taking a seat on the sofa, she turns on the TV.

If she thinks her usually silent and collected little sister would drop the topic, she is in for a shock.

I'm too protective of her to leave her alone to stew.

I'm going to turn myself into Emily's version. I can be stubborn too. After all, I learned from the best.

I stomp over and stand in front of her with my hands planted on my hips. "Why did you call in sick when you are absolutely fine?"

"You're blocking my view, Ro." She grumbles and I suppress my smile.

"I'm not giving up until you start talking." Folding my arms over my chest, I tap my right foot repetitively on the ground for good measure. All the while keeping my expressions in check.

"I didn't feel like going and I didn't take a single day off since I have started working at T&A, so it's not a big deal." She rolls her eyes.

"Okay, fair enough. Do you have any possible explanation about why you are so fidgety this morning?"

"I'm not fidgety." She glares at me.

I remain silent and stare pointedly at her knee which is bouncing up and down; a telltale of anxiousness.

She stops the movement with a hand and her shoulders slump. Her beautiful blonde locks fall over her face, almost hiding her sadness.

I drop the tough act and move to sit beside her and take her hands in mine.

"You wanna talk about it?" I murmur softly.

She is lost in her thoughts again. It's like looking in the mirror. I have been in this state myself.

Nobody could see my turmoil. Because I have always been the silent type. Emotionally guarded.

Emily on the other hand is like the brightest sun rays.

No matter where you are, it shines on you. Gives you warmth and brings a content smile to your face.

One could easily tell if she's happy or sad because she wears her heart on her sleeve.

Right now, I know something is bugging her. I can't have the gray clouds of dejection conceal her sunshine.

At the stretched silence, I ask, "Is this about Asher?"

She lets out a groan and leans back against the couch.

"I'll take that as a yes. So, what has Asher done that forced you into hiding away from him?"

"I'm not hiding!" I smile at that. There's that small hint of the real Emily. Almost there.

"Are too." I tease, bumping my shoulder against hers.

"Rochelle!"

"Emily."

We stare at each other for a few seconds before giving into the urge to laugh.

When our laughter recedes, she starts talking.

She opens up and starts reciting everything from the very beginning.

It's like she has been bottling up her emotions for so long, she has finally reached her limits, and it's all surfacing.

She tells me everything that went down with her boss yesterday. How he confessed about wanting her. And how the moment was broken by his brother's arrival.

She was so nervous to face him that she took the day off.

"Do you like him?" I ask her in all seriousness.

"He's infuriating… and cocky." She dodges my question and understandably so.

It must be difficult to admit you have feelings for the person you have always claimed of hating.

"Answer me, Emily. It's a simple yes or no question. If you don't like him, you should be upfront about it and I'm sure he would stop his advancements. You running away is confusing him, don't you think?"

"What if I do like him?" she mutters. Her face turns bright pink.

"Then I think you should tell him. It is always better than living with regrets." I smile wryly. "If you do decide on making a move, be careful. I don't want you to get hurt."

With that, I get up and head to the kitchen.

To clean the messy counter and also to keep *my* emotions buried deep within.

CHAPTER 3

Rochelle

Growing up, I have always been pampered by my family. I lived a sheltered life being the youngest. That meant being the apple of my parents' eyes.

When I used to live with my parents in Brooklyn, life was peaceful.

My routine mostly included school, libraries, cooking, and sometimes a stroll alone in the park with a box of my favorite chocolate chip cookies.

My folks never forced me to do anything. This was the life I chose for myself—however simple it may seem.

Emily on the other hand was pretty tough since the beginning.

She started working part-time jobs in her early teens and soon moved here to Manhattan when she got the opportunity.

When it was time to apply for colleges, I applied for NYU and was ecstatic to receive the acceptance letter.

As soon as Serah moved out, I had a conversation with Emily about the living arrangement I had in mind.

Instead of living on campus, I opted for moving into the spare bedroom of Emily's basement apartment.

I have never lived on my own before let alone with strangers.

The idea of living in a dorm with a stranger was uncomfortable.

Mom, Dad, and Emily tried to change my mind. They wanted me to experience college life but I reasoned with them.

I simply wasn't cut out for that kind of life. Parties and all are not something I saw myself indulging in. Also, there was a strong point of saving the expenses.

Moving in with my sister felt right. She welcomed me with open arms.

Just because I was now living with my sister didn't mean I could just mooch off her.

Before moving in, I made myself clear about my contributions to the household. I wanted to be independent.

Hence, the café gig. I never knew working could be such an enlightening experience.

Whenever I ride the subway alone or when I'm simply walking through the crowd on the busy sidewalk, a sense of independence envelops me.

The feeling of freedom. I can't express it in words. I feel like *somebody*. Like I matter.

I love what I do.

Who would've thought I would enjoy interacting with people and serving them beverages?

But I don't claim the job is easy. It isn't. Standing for hours on end is no joke.

I'm lucky the owners of the café—*Sip of Joy*—are great people.

The old couple was patient with my inexperienced self and overlooked a few mishaps on my part.

In a few days, it'll be a month since I joined.

I quickly change into my black top with the café logo and tie the apron over it.

With my usual rag tugged in the back pocket of my sky-blue jeans, I quickly tie my dark brown hair in a high ponytail.

I left Emily with her snacks and promised to make the cinnamon rolls some other day. I have an afternoon shift so I had no time for it.

Actually, I insisted on this shift.

I was meant to work in the evening today but I convinced my co-worker to let me work the noon hours.

The man with chocolate eyes came by around one in the afternoon yesterday. I want to be present in case he decides to show up again.

I know keeping unwarranted expectations may lead to disappointments, but having hope makes my heart calm.

And as Colette, the French author said, *hope costs nothing.*

He never came.

Seconds turned to minutes. Minutes to hours.

It's three p.m. now and I am currently occupying a seat by the glass wall, overlooking the people passing by.

I am on a ten-minute break. I close my eyes and take a deep breath, the aroma of coffee beans filling my nostrils.

"One Espresso, please." I open my eyes at that. My head swirls in the direction of the counter and finds a man in a suit.

A man who's not *him*.

I shake my head with a somber smile.

I take a bite of the cookie and it somehow lifts my spirit. There's nothing a homemade chocolate chip cookie can't fix.

I still have five minutes left. I take unhurried sips of my cold coffee and think about college.

It is still a month away. I have already decided on the electives and what path I have to take for my career.

It's all set and discussed with my family. But sometimes… I wish…

A tap on my shoulders startles me.

"Oh, Mr. Taylor." I calm my heartbeats and rest the cup on the table.

"I didn't mean to startle you, Ms. Moore." He gives me an apologetic smile and takes a seat opposite mine.

"Rochelle please." I smile.

"Then you have to call me Michael." His eyes crinkle at the corner.

It's a running joke between us. He is accustomed to my habit of always calling him Mr. Taylor. So, he came up with the idea of calling me "Ms. Moore" because I don't like it.

His white hair is slicked back and he's wearing a suit.

Mr. Taylor is one of our regulars. He is seventy-something years old and usually stops by for his dose of caffeine after his morning walks.

He is the first friend I made here. He never visits at this time though. So seeing him here is kind of a surprise.

"I'll get your usual right away." I smile and move to get up but he stops me.

"I have already placed the order, dear." He gives me a soft smile. But his eyes lack the usual gleam in them. It looks somewhat sad.

"Everything okay, Michael?"

"Yes. Just had a meeting which went on for hours. Drained my energy." He sighs.

"Try this. I made them." I slide my small plastic container of cookies toward him.

He leans forward and picks one. He takes a bite. Then another. He chews slowly, a contemplating look crosses over his face.

"Well?"

"Hmm." He polishes off the cookie in the third bite.

"Michael?" I ask with a small voice.

He swallows and breaks into a huge grin. "It's the best cookie I have ever tasted." He takes another one.

I release the breath I was holding and chuckle lightly.

"Now, that's a bit of a stretch." I may not know much about him but I know he comes from money. And men like him travel often which means a plethora of opportunities to taste finer delicacies.

"Trust me when I say this, you have a knack for baking."

He says this because this isn't the first time he has tasted something I baked. I had surprised him with a little box of blueberry muffins a week ago along with his coffee.

I give him a gentle smile with a hint of pride.

We chat for a few more minutes. I get up before he could when his order gets called.

I place his iced tea in front of him and raise an eyebrow before taking a seat. He usually orders espresso or Americano.

"The heat is stifling today. Can you blame me?" He rolls his eyes and I laugh softly.

"As I was saying, you must go to a culinary school. You are clearly passionate about cooking, why not go for it?"

The smile I was still wearing falters.

"I can't." I stare at the brick wall behind him.

Some things are easier said than done. I shake myself internally before pursing my lips.

"Besides, I have decided I want to go for business management."

"I don't understand. I thought you must be interested in pursuing a career in culinary arts." he regards me with his brows furrowed.

"Me too," I mutter to myself. "But as I said, I have all things mapped out for me." I reach for my drink and take a healthy sip.

"Okay." He says as he sips his tea.

I don't like the silence so I blurt, "I am looking for an internship right now."

"Oh?"

"Yes, while this gig is great, I am looking for hands-on experience in managing business operations."

Michael appears deep in thoughts at that. But before I could question it, Maria, my co-worker calls out my name.

I glance at my wristwatch and realize my break is long over.

Oh, no. "Michael, I gotta head back." I give him a wave before heading to the counter.

CHAPTER 4

Three weeks later

Alan

Just as I'm reaching the lights, the touchscreen on the dashboard of my tesla indicates an incoming call.

Stopping the car, I answer by tapping on the screen. "Hello, brother."

"Alan, where are you? You're twenty minutes late." His voice booms through the speakers and echoes in the close confinements of the car.

"I'm driving. I'll be there in ten." I say as I navigate the route which would lead me to the place I couldn't stop thinking about.

"Don't tell me you just left your office." He growls.

"You're prolonging my arrival by talking," I respond dryly. He breathes out a bark of disbelief.

I park at the curb when I arrive at the destination and reach inside the chest pocket of my jacket.

My fingers find what I am looking for and retrieve it to gaze at it.

I breathe in deep as I trace the dainty silver bracelet with a heart charm in the centre.

It's been *days* since the girl with the most enchanting green eyes left me with a souvenir.

Twenty-two days to be exact.

It was not until I was out of the café and inside my car that I noticed her silver bracelet tangled in my sweater.

Am I here to return this bracelet to its owner? Or am I here for something more? I have no idea.

Sip of Joy. I read the name of the café again. This is where I saw her.

I don't know what it is about this girl because I am unable to keep her out of my head.

Even the endless meetings regarding my ongoing acquisition couldn't manage to wrench her thoughts away.

I thought with the days passing, and the piling work, I would forget about her.

And when I continued to dream of those emerald eyes, I knew I had to see her.

"Well, I'm going to stop by a café… do you want anything?"

"No. We've got everything covered. Emily has prepared the menu keeping everyone's favourites in mind. Including yours. So don't hurt her feelings. Just show up."

My tone gentles. "Okay."

Emily is a sweet girl. I've met her and I get why Asher—the man with commitment issues—fell head over heels for her.

She is the kind of girl who could make you laugh on your bad days. She is good for my idiot brother.

I must hurry up. I would hate to dampen her mood. I exit the car and lock it before heading towards the coffee shop.

As I am taking each step, I notice the acceleration of my heartbeats. My palms feel clammy as I step inside.

I have been in company with powerful men since a young age and still can't recall the last time I was this flurried.

I stay rooted in the threshold and scan the surroundings. The place is packed.

Everyone is busy in their own world.

I don't know why I am prolonging but I can't look in the direction of the counter just yet.

After a minute, I finally glance at the counter.

The girl behind the counter is facing away from me. In a second, I conclude, the girl working there isn't *her*.

I have seen her only once but her petite little frame starred in my dreams so many times that I knew this girl isn't the one I am looking for.

Still, I wait. And when she does turn around, my prediction is proven accurate.

Disappointment crashes over me.

I wait for a few more minutes to catch the signs of her.

When there's still no trace of her, I turn around and leave.

With a defeated sigh, I resume the place behind the wheel.

I'm already late for the brunch, Asher would have my head if I delay one more second.

The lift opens to Asher's penthouse.

A few steps in and I see Emily sprinting towards me.

"You made it." she breathes as she comes to a halt.

"Emily, you look lovely. Thank you for inviting me." I hand her the flowers I bought on the way here.

"OH! Thank you! Please come in. Everyone's in the solarium." She grins.

"After you."

We cross the living room and head in the direction of the solarium.

Throughout the way, Emily talks about the brunch. I silently listen to her chatter.

She is a great girl. The purpose of this brunch was to cheer Lexi up.

From the brief conversation with Asher yesterday, I came to know that Lexi—who's an old friend of Asher's—has been living at his penthouse for the last three days.

Asher brought her to his place the night she was physically abused by her husband.

Even after knowing Asher had a history with Lexi, Emily has been nothing but supportive instead of feeling insecure.

Emily took Lexi under her wing and moved in temporarily to be there for her during her stay. And arranged this get-together for her.

That earned Emily more respect from me.

"Finally, Alan has graced us with his presence, people!" I hear Asher's voice from my right as Emily and I step inside the sunlit room.

"Sarcasm doesn't become you, brother..." My voice trails when I turn in his direction.

Something moves inside my chest at the sight of someone beside him.

The afternoon light streaming in the room through the glass walls and high ceilings is creating an illusion of a dream.

The dream-like state of the atmosphere isn't providing enough clarity and is making it impossible to believe what I am seeing.

Am I dreaming with my eyes open?

I squint and sure enough, there she is.

The girl I was searching for in the coffee shop earlier.

The girl I had in my arms three weeks ago.

The girl with forest green eyes.

As I stand in the room staring at her, everything fades away.

My senses go numb and all I can do is focus on *her*.

I don't blink, afraid of breaking this moment in case this is not real. But she is very much real. Still here.

She takes a sharp intake of air. And it is then I realise that she is just as affected as I am.

"Do you two know each other?" A voice breaks the moment and I jerk a little.

Asher's inquisitive gaze is pinned on me. Like he asked a question.

Oh, yes, he did.

Before I could form a response, Emily—who's still standing beside me—speaks. "You know my sister?"

I gaze at her stunned expression. It takes a few seconds for her words to register.

Sister.

The girl who I was searching for is Emily's sister?

I'm suddenly hit with a memory from a few days ago.

"Are you planning on finishing anytime soon?" Asher asks in an exasperated tone.

I look up at him. "I told you I can't make it, brother. I still have to go through these." I motion at the pile of files sitting on the mahogany desk.

His face falls and I feel like shit.

He's been making efforts to spend time with me.

I make a quick mental note to update my schedule so I could attend weekly dinners with him and Emily.

I glance at the small plastic box in his hand. To lighten up his mood, I ask, "Is that for me?"

He looks down at the box and grins before looking back at me. "No way. Rochelle made these cookies specifically for me."

At the mention of a girl, I raise an eyebrow.

"She is Emily's sister, dickhead." He rolls his eyes.

I just blink at him.

"I am a changed man. I am taken. Besides, Rochelle is only eighteen. She's practically a kid!"

My lips twitch at his adamant tone. Who knew Asher could be so in love?

"Okay, Mr. Changed Man, it's better that you head back. Didn't you tell me Emily is home and mustn't be left alone with an accessible kitchen?"

He stands swiftly, the guest chair rocks with the force. "I should go."

I chuckle as he leaves my office in a hurry.

"Send them up." Asher's clipped tone snaps me out of my trance.

"What's wrong?" Tatum, Asher's business partner, and his only close friend asks.

I watch with numb silence as Asher informs everyone that Colin, Lexi's husband is here with his lawyer.

There's panic in Lexi's eyes and everyone seems stressed. Her entire body is stiff.

Lexi has suffered trauma because of her husband. Who would want to face the person who reminds you of something horrible?

"I apologise, everyone. But I think it's best if you all leave. I don't want to drag you all in this." Asher looks at us.

"We are staying," Tatum says, and I nod in agreement.

"But the ladies should go," I suggest Asher while keeping my eyes trained on Rochelle who's huddled against Lexi, comforting her.

The need to protect her from the impending danger takes root in me.

Her eyes lift and collide with mine.

"We are not going anywhere." Tatum's wife, Serah says and Rochelle nods.

I scowl.

Rochelle doesn't understand. The man who's about to enter is an accused who could be dangerous even with us present here.

The ladies must steer clear of the confrontation that's going to take place with the men coming up.

I am about to object but swallow the words when we are all ushered out of the solarium and into the living room where the two men are already waiting.

This day has already turned out to be a shocker. I have no clue what's going to happen now, but whatever it is, I'm not going to leave my brother's side.

And now I have one more person to look after.

My eyes follow Rochelle as she takes small steps towards the sofa and takes a seat beside the ladies.

She is eighteen.

I wrench my eyes away from her at that reminder. She is too young.

There's a good seven-year age gap between us. I have to forget about her even if it would test my limits.

Especially now that I know her name and how to get to her, staying away from her is going to be an arduous task.

Rochelle

My savior's name is Alan.

SINFUL LOVE

Ever since the day he saved me at the café, I have been working only afternoon shifts in the hopes of catching a glimpse of him.

When days after days passed, the last bit of hope of ever seeing him withered away.

It's like that encounter never happened.

I consoled my heart by convincing it that the day he came into my life was all a dream.

Time was a great ally in distracting me from the thoughts of him.

But then, I saw him today. And every feeling and emotion I chased away in the past weeks came hurtling toward me.

I saw him a minute before his eyes landed on me.

I thought I was imagining it all until he locked those dark eyes on me. I felt immobilized by the intensity they contained.

Hope rekindled within me when I saw a flash of recognition in his gaze.

Before I could do anything, the moment had ended.

Lexi's husband caused a scene that had Asher say some questionable things to Emily.

The person whom she loved with all her heart and soul broke her within seconds.

My heart ached for my sister when she sprinted out of Asher's penthouse.

Serah and I followed suit. Tatum drove us back to our apartment.

Now it is just me and Emily. Serah and Tatum left shortly after as Emily wanted to be alone.

I respected her decision and left her alone but I desperately want to go inside her bedroom and hug her. But I know she needs time to process.

Unable to sit still, I get up from the living room couch and head to the kitchen.

I tighten the ponytail and fetch my apron.

I'm going to make Emily's favorite strawberry tart with whipped cream.

This wouldn't lessen her heartache but it's the only way I could comfort her.

As I set to work, I can't help but think about Alan.

I remember Emily mentioning Asher's younger brother on numerous occasions but I failed to put two and two together.

Their accent was a huge tell. And now that I have seen them together, there's no denying that the two are brothers.

The similarities are easy to spot.

They both have jet-black hair. They share a striking resemblance. Such as their strong cheekbones, the same sharp jawline, perfect eyebrows, and eyelashes that would make any girl jealous.

The only difference is, Asher always has a mischievous grin on his face and Alan…. well, it's only the second time I saw him, but it was apparent he was completely opposite of his brother.

He gives off a serious vibe.

I'm sprinkling sugar on the puff pastry and strawberries when the doorbell rings.

Quickly discarding the apron, I reach the door to answer it.

When I open the door, my mood sours.

Asher's grim face greets me. My eyes slide to his hand.

He's carrying a…. chocolate bouquet in his hand.

He sure knows Emily and her love for chocolates.

He looks out of sorts and jittery. I might have found it funny or sweet even on any other day, but not today.

Emily's tear-soaked face is still fresh in my mind and the reason behind her state is standing in front of me.

My expression turns stern and with steel in my voice, I say, "Now's not the right time, Asher."

I start to close the door but he prevents it with his free hand.

"I'm sorry." He mutters and barges inside.

I watch with stunned silence as he strides in the direction of Emily's room.

I stand rooted in place for what feels like ages then shake myself internally and start toward her room.

I am almost there when I hear them.

"Asher, what are you doing?"

"Please hear me out." His voice is dripping with anguish.

If she says she doesn't want to see him, I'll escort him out.

I wait for Emily's decision.

"Please, baby." Asher pleads; his tone desperate with thick emotions.

I leave them alone when Emily agrees on listening to what he has to say.

CHAPTER 5

A week later

Rochelle

I'm scrolling through the emails on the phone and mostly find junk. I've applied to a few companies for the internship and so far only succeeded in snagging phone interviews.

With a sigh, I dig into my jeans pocket for the apartment keys.

I'm cracking my neck as I push the door open and a flurry of blonde locks catches me off guard.

"RO, YOU'RE BACK!" Emily's arms encircle me in a tight hug.

I catch a breath before hugging her back. She is a ball of energy when happy.

A lot has happened in the past week.

After the day Asher barged into our apartment *with* a chocolate bouquet, might I add, Emily asked for some time and space to think.

That didn't deter him. He started dropping off her favorite food every day following their talk. Each takeout bag contained sweet handwritten notes by him.

Emily acted tough but it didn't last long and they were back together.

I assumed she would be at his place like last night but I am pleased to find her here now.

"Someone's happy to see me." I tease after pulling away.

"Of course, I am. It's like we haven't spent time together at all in ages." She pouts.

I couldn't agree more. With my café shift and her job, we hardly get time to catch up.

And she has been spending the nights at Asher's. I have missed our movie nights.

"You're here now. We could watch a movie tonight." I suggest as we walk into the living room.

"I would love to," I could sense a 'but' coming. She continues. "but I'm going out for dinner with Asher."

I plop on the couch with a sigh. She sits beside me and wraps an arm around my shoulders. "*and…* you are coming." Emily adds.

"I can't. I am so tired." I really am. And I don't wish to spend the night being the third wheel.

"I don't want to hear it, missy. You're coming with me. I already have dresses ready to wear for tonight."

"A dress?" My eyebrows jump as she nods eagerly and sprints to her bedroom.

I am still wide-eyed as she enters the living room with a dress in each hand.

"What do you think?" she wags her eyebrows.

The beige midi dress looks every bit elegant. So does the other dress.

It's a solid black A-line split dress. Unlike the beige number; which has a turtle neck design, this one has a sweetheart neckline.

"I must say, you have a great wardrobe, Em." I eye the short black dress longingly.

Regardless of it being slightly revealing, I desire to try it.

I don't own many dresses, much less a revealing one. I would've happily tagged along with them for that dress alone. But I am dead tired.

Right now, all I want is a long bath and then a book to spend the rest of the evening.

"I know, right?" she mimics Regina George and I can't help but chuckle with her.

"Come on, Ro! We are going to be late." She twirls, flailing the dresses that are hanging from her outstretched arms.

I let out a soft laugh. "I wish I could but I don't have the strength to go out tonight. I'm beat."

I get up and pinch her cheeks when her smile falls. "Besides, you'll have Asher all to yourself. We both know how territorial he gets when it comes to your attention. I don't want to fight him for yours." I joke.

She grins at that. "You won't have to. As Alan is joining us too."

Something stills within me at the mention of his name.

My fatigue is forgotten, a new surge of energy courses through my limbs. A foreign feeling. Excitement. It melts away my exhaustion and fills me with eagerness.

This might be my only chance to see him again. I would be lying to myself if I said I wasn't disappointed that Alan didn't reach out to me.

It only meant he didn't feel the connection *I* did on our first encounter.

For him, I might be just a café barista. But for me, he is something vital.

I am unaware of the roots of these feelings or what to name these emotions I have for him—a person I hardly know.

But one thing is clear, whenever I am in close vicinity with him, I feel this strong pull toward him that I have never experienced before.

So even if I know he doesn't view me in that same light, I crave to catch a glimpse of him, however brief it may be.

I need it.

Calming my heartbeats, I ask, "Which dress are you wearing?"

"Does that mean you're coming?" Her green eyes sparkle with enthusiasm.

I nod with a shy smile.

"YES!" she bounces up and down for a good minute before adding, "I'm going with the beige. It accentuates my curves."

That means the dress I loved so much is mine for the night. She hands it to me and I start toward my bedroom, hugging the dress to my chest.

"Don't move!" Emily glares at me.

"Is this necessary?" I watch her with one eye as she applies eyeliner on the other.

I asked her to do my light makeup as I don't know the first thing about cosmetics.

Emily being the queen of makeup was thrilled and immediately ran to her room to get her makeup kit.

After doing my eyes, she moves to my lips and applies one of her matte lipsticks.

"Take a look." She steps back and I stand from the chair she dragged in the bathroom for me to sit.

A gasp emits from my lips. I gaze at the mirror but don't see myself.

No, the girl staring back at me isn't the eighteen-year-old timid girl who always dresses in tees and jeans.

The reflection I am looking at right now is not of a teenage girl. She is all… woman.

My silky dark brown mane cascades down past the shoulders, my eyes shimmer with the glittery matte eye shadow she applied on them.

The eye shadow color she chose is so light it gives a natural look and highlights my green eyes. Especially with the liner, they look more enhanced.

The nude color she painted my lips with completes my look.

The thought of Alan seeing me all dolled up sends shivers down my spine.

The dress fits me perfectly and I can't help the giddiness.

I turn to Emily and squeeze her in an embrace. "Thank you. I love it."

"Anytime." She hugs me back with equal force.

We are still locked in an embrace when her phone goes off. She pulls away and checks it.

"It's Asher. I guess he's here." She dashes out of the bathroom to attend the call.

I turn my head and watch myself in the mirror one more time.

Its time. Time to finally see him.

Suddenly shy of my own reflection, I avert my eyes. My heart is racing and I place a hand over my chest to calm it.

What's going to happen to you when he sees us? I ask my eager heart.

"Ro, let's go. He is waiting outside!" Emily's excited voice reaches me. With a deep breath, I step out.

We spot Asher's black Aston Martin DB11 parked across the street.

He is leaning against the car, his attention occupied by the phone in his hand as we approach him.

He straightens when he sees us.

Asher's honey-colored eyes go soft as Emily wraps her arms around his neck for a kiss.

"I missed you." He says against her lips.

Emily giggles. "You saw me this afternoon."

"So? Can't I miss my girlfriend?" He goes for another kiss and I avert my eyes, my cheeks heating by their PDA.

The fingers of my right hand close on my left wrist to play with the bracelet. I stop the hand. It might take some time to let go of the habit of reaching out for my bracelet.

I look for him. Is he inside the car?

"Rochelle," I glance at Asher who is now standing beside me.

Emily is already seated in the passenger seat.

Asher opens the door to the backseat. I get in and find the back seat empty.

I vaguely register him shutting the door behind me and rounding the car to take the seat behind the wheels.

Alan is not here. As if Emily gets the telepathic message, she asks, "Where's Alan?"

I hold my breath and shift to the edge of the seat to listen.

"I got his message a few minutes ago. He's running late and will meet us there directly."

I release the pent-up breath I was holding.

He'll be there. My heart settles after hearing it.

"We should order starters while we wait," Asher speaks in a dejected tone.

It's been more than fifteen minutes since we arrived. There's still no sign of Alan.

"Let's wait. It is not polite to start without him. I'm not that hungry." Her stomach growls loudly, betraying her words.

Asher and I start chuckling despite the somber mood his brother's absence put us in.

According to Emily, Asher was looking forward to having dinner with his brother.

That makes two of us.

Emily turns beet-red and glances around before shooting daggers at us. "I hate you both."

"You blush beautifully." Asher caresses her cheek with a finger.

"And you change the topic tactfully." She pokes his bicep with a finger.

"Ow, you hurt me." Asher mocks. They start bickering and I shake my head with a small smile on my lips.

Asher orders a few beverages.

My eyes sweep over the beautiful chandelier in the middle of the ceiling.

It's rectangular with small glowing bulbs. It is bathing the hall in fluorescent light.

The ambiance of this place is soothing with soft music.

Yet all I am left with is hopeless despair.

The dress I was so eager to wear holds no interest at this moment. I garnered the attention of handsome men when we entered the dining area of the restaurant.

But the one person I wanted to notice all this isn't present.

A gasp from the nearby table attracts my eyes toward them.

The women sitting at the table are watching the entryway of the hall with eagerness.

I avoid them and return to my dreadful thoughts.

My eyes roam aimlessly through the surroundings.

Another group of females a few tables over are glancing at the entryway, which is directly behind me.

I frown. What's so intriguing which had almost all the women here to avoid their dates?

SINFUL LOVE

Should I turn my head to see what all the fuss is about?

I eye the lovebirds who are completely unaware of the world and are in their bubble.

Curiosity gets the best of me. I start turning my head but before I could look, a shadow falls over me.

"Is this seat taken?" a deep voice asks, weakening my lungs to draw another breath.

CHAPTER 6

Rochelle

"Alan, fucking finally." I watch as Asher stands to hug his brother.

From my peripheral vision, I see the women who were gawking at the entryway with keen interest a minute ago are now staring at Alan.

Oh, so he was the one they were so openly ogling.

"Your vocabulary is ever so colorful," Alan says in a dry tone as he pulls away.

He gives a quick hug to Emily before taking a seat beside me.

"Rochelle." He nods.

I squeak a hello in response without looking at him.

What's wrong, Rochelle? You agreed to this evening because it promised his company.

And now when he is right beside you, why are you punishing yourself by denying your eyes to get their fill of him?

I pick my glass of sparkling water and take a sip. Anything to appear collected when I am anything but.

"First, I'd like to apologise to everyone," Alan says and my grip on the glass tightens.

My eyes betray me and slide in his direction.

He is even more breathtakingly beautiful up close.

I take in his side profile and find myself leaning toward him ever so slightly. I am so grateful he is not looking at me right now.

I take advantage of the opportunity and just look at him.

Really look at him. His hair is slightly ruffled like he's been raking his fingers through it in frustration.

I remember noticing how his hair was styled neatly on the last two times I saw him.

For some reason, Alan seems like a man who likes everything in order, and finding his hair in disarray bugs me.

I want to reach inside his head and find out what is wrong.

I want to know what's bothering him so I could erase his worries.

Now that I am looking at him, his features are dulled with exhaustion.

I hear Asher asking him about the reason for his delay.

"There was a situation at work that required my attention. Anyway, let's not discuss work and make this evening insipid, brother." Alan's lips twitch. But it doesn't bloom into a full smile.

Alan's aura is all serious and stern. I wonder then, what would he look like while smiling.

My eyes drag to his full lips and try to picture him smiling.

How would it look like?

How would his smile *taste* like?

The thought is so wrong, I feel guilty.

I jerk my eyes up and everything in me stills when I find him looking right at me.

Seconds pass and I think I'll die out of mortification.

"Ro? Do you want to order something else?" Emily asks. I look at her with furrowed brows. What is she talking about?

"Huh?"

"Alan asked you a question. What would you like to have? Burrata or tortellini?"

I blink back the confusion and notice the server standing by our table.

"I'll have B-burrata, please. T-thank you." I clamp my mouth shut after that stuttering disaster.

I feel Alan's eyes on me but I ignore them and concentrate on the dish being served.

Why? Just why did I have to get caught while staring at him? Why is he so darn handsome that I can't take my eyes off of him?

I made a fool out of myself in front of everyone.

Absentmindedly, I cut into the burrata. The creaminess content oozes out in the process. I take a bite.

As soon as I close my lips around the fork, flavors burst on my tongue.

Cheese along with orange dressing drizzled on the burrata melts on my tongue and I close my eyes.

Savoring the taste, I moan. The blend of cheese, kalamata olives, and citrus coating of orange are making the burrata all the more scrumptious.

I lick my lips.

"That good?"

My lids fly open at the question. Alan's gaze is trained on my lips.

My heart flips as it stays there. I bite my lip, my face heating up at his stare.

Alan slowly lifts his eyes and it meets mine. There's a sheen of…. heat in them. Or am I imagining it?

"Yes." I hold his gaze, even when every fiber of my being is on fire.

My breathing turns shallow when he remains silent. The more he stares at me, the more my heart gets hopeful.

Is that desire I am seeing in his eyes or is it a mere reflection of mine?

I got more than I bargained for tonight.

Not only have I got to see him, but I also managed to hold his attention.

A phone rings, startling us enough to break the eye contact.

And just like that, the spell breaks.

I sneak a glance at Emily and Asher and find them murmuring to each other with goofy smiles.

That means they didn't notice us having a staring contest seconds ago.

"Excuse me." Alan motions to his phone that's still going off and stands.

After he leaves in the direction of the hallway across the room, I can't help but wonder about the person calling him.

Is that his girlfriend? I shake my head internally.

Whatever he does or whomever he dates shouldn't be your concern, Rochelle.

But I care. My heart whispers.

Too bad we can't do anything about it, heart.

I concentrate on the delectable dish and take another forkful.

I am polishing off the last of the burrata when Alan returns and resumes his seat.

"What was that about?" Asher asks by nodding at the phone Alan is still gripping.

"My assistant, Olivia called to inform me about the travelling arrangements for the next week."

"Are you going somewhere?"

"I am just going to explore the properties in case the current acquisition fails. I should have plan B ready."

"You can sue him for backing out of the deal, yes?" Asher frowns.

"Legally, no. He didn't sign anything to make it official. So, I am going to look for properties here for Will's Valley. By hook or by crook, I am going to open a branch of my hotel here. Even if I have to start with the whole process again." He says with a grim tone. "At least I have reliable staff to carry on my overseas business smoothly."

"Speaking of business," Asher looks at me then. "Aren't you opting for a business major, Rochelle?"

"Yes. Business management."

"Emily told me you were looking for an internship program."

I don't know what to make out of this sudden change in the course of the conversation. But I answer regardless.

"Yeah... I gave a few phone interviews but so far, I didn't receive any callbacks."

"Why don't you take her in as your intern?" Asher asks Alan.

I look at Asher in shock, mouth agape. Alan seems to be stunned at the suggestion too, given the stillness of his body.

"My office only has eight employees. As we are still settling here, we don't have a requirement for additional staff."

His words are direct and I won't lie, it hurt.

"You said you're going to explore properties. Take her with you on every site. She'll get the hands-on experience on business management and could gain knowledge by witnessing how the process of acquisition unfolds."

Alan is still silent and I don't think I could bear any more humiliation than this.

Of course, I lack experience, but I didn't ask Asher for his help.

However, he has my deepest gratitude, but I can't let him speak for me.

If I wanted to be a charity case, I would have asked Asher for an internship at T&A.

I open my mouth to express my disagreement when Alan speaks.

"I think you are right. We could use an extra hand in the coming schedule."

"But—"

Alan turns to me. His commanding eyes demand my silence. "No buts, Rochelle. I'll see you in my office on Monday."

While this could be a great opportunity for my career, I dread the days I would be spending with Alan.

Having a crush on my sister's boyfriend's brother was bad enough, how am I going to work if the said crush will be my *boss?*

CHAPTER 7

Rochelle

"How do I look?" I ask in a timorous voice.

"Who are you and what have you done to my Ro?" her eyes sweep over the outfit I picked for the first day of my internship.

It's a simple yet professional-looking olive-green twill skirt that ends inches above my knee.

I paired it with an off-white button-down shirt that's tucked into the skirt. I finished the outfit with cream-colored pointy toe Stiletto Pumps.

The extra three inches is a good boost to my five feet three height.

I felt confident when I went shopping with Emily yesterday but now as I have these clothes on, I am a ball of nerves.

So, I went to the person who's my number one cheerleader. My big sister.

She was blow-drying her hair in front of the dresser when I entered her room.

She abandoned the task and turned swiftly when she caught my reflection in the mirror.

When I remain silent and fidgety, she reaches me in three big steps and grips my shoulders.

"You look so beautiful, Ro. You *are* beautiful. But now you're looking like a grownup!" she hugs me and I breathe in her familiar scent.

"Are you ready to enter into the business world, kiddo?" she asks after pulling away.

I shake my head no but say, "Yes."

That makes her laugh. "Remember how nervous you were on your first day at the café?"

I nod.

"You ended up loving it, right?"

I did. Only because it included me making drinks. I enjoyed learning about varieties of drinks and how to make them. Through that job, I was able to do something I loved.

When I nod again, she continues, "You'll fit right in. I know any type of change in routine makes you anxious, but this is life, kiddo. And let's not forget, you'll have Alan. He's a part of our family too."

That's the issue. The thought of seeing him on a daily basis is making me jittery.

Since the dinner two days ago, I have been beating myself up for not speaking up when they were talking on my behalf.

With his one command, Alan rendered me speechless.

I almost called Asher to tell him that I don't want the internship.

But then the logical part of me stopped me from doing so.

This is an opportunity and I should be grateful that I received it without any hassle. The least I could do is accept it and work hard to prove my worth.

So even if I am anxious, I am going to face my fears and try my level best to not make Alan regret giving me this chance.

"Yeah."

"And don't forget to make friends. Mingle with your colleagues. Don't be your shy self. I don't want you to be a loner." She gives me a meaningful look.

I bob my head. "I prepared sandwiches and packed extra for my co-workers. I hope this way I could connect with them." I give her a shy smile.

This is the only way I know how to communicate. Through food.

I am not that great at holding an interesting conversation. At least by doing this, I can extend a hand of friendship.

"You're so sweet, Ro. This world doesn't deserve you." She kisses the crown of my head, making my heart smile.

Alan's office is located in Midtown Manhattan. My hands are sweaty as I crane my neck to take in the skyscraper.

So it begins. Once I enter the building, there's no backing out.

I had to quit the café gig. My college starts in four days. My time would be divided between the internship and my classes.

That means it's time to let go of my dream of going to culinary school. Sometimes, I can't help but wonder how different my current situation would have been if I had courage.

Courage to tell my family that I want to follow my passion instead of following in my sister's footsteps. They would have supported me had I been honest with them.

But they were so proud of Emily and I couldn't help but be envious of her. There's a lot of competition in the field I want to be in. But each sector, each field of career has it.

Debating with myself at this point is simply pointless. This is a new beginning for me and I have to embrace it.

With a deep breath, I head inside.

The elevator door opens on the twenty-second floor, giving the view of open space.

I step out and spot the reception desk at the end of the room. I approach the receptionist and introduce myself.

She gives me directions and I follow them.

Walking through the intimidating hallway, I turn left.

The open floor office is spacious. It contains cubicles alongside offices lining the edges.

What's odd is that there's no one present here as far as I can see. I walk further and find only vacant chairs and pin-drop silence.

I frown. Should I check out every room here or head back to the reception desk to enquire about the whereabouts of the employees?

I should ask the receptionist. With a nod, I turn around to walk back in the direction I came from but my head collides with a strong chest.

A man's chest.

Before I could apologize for my clumsiness, my heels stumble and my hands take purchase in whatever they can find—the lapels of his suit jacket.

Two brawny arms surround my back. The warmth of the splayed palms on the expanse of my back commands my eyes to snap up.

"Alan." I gasp.

"Rochelle." He takes in my features with concerned eyes before asking, "Are you all right?"

No, I am not. You have me in your arms with your chest against mine. I can feel the heat your body is oozing out and my pulse is going haywire as I can breathe your clean, masculine scent.

I feel almost dizzy with sensation overload. So, no. I am *not* all right.

"Y-yes," I clear my throat and ease the death grip on his lapels. "Sorry." I am not certain why I am apologizing.

For crashing into him? For having such reactions to his proximity? For not getting over my crush? I don't know.

I stare at his perfect tie knot instead of his eyes, hoping he wouldn't catch the disappointment in my gaze at the thought of losing his touch any second now. I wait for him to release me.

Seconds pass and when he's still holding onto me, I peer up at him.

Alan is staring at me with an unreadable look.

I start squirming against him with each passing second.

Not because I am uncomfortable. No. It's because his eyes are beginning to converse with me. They are telling me something I want *him* to say.

The need to be even closer to him courses through me.

Even with heels, I barely reach to his chin so I push on my toes, my eyes never leaving his. I swallow before licking my lips.

Seeing my face inches away from him seems to snap him back to reality.

Alan straightens and takes a step back, causing me to wobble again.

His hand reaches out to steady me but before it could connect with me, I steady myself and step away.

He can't just play with my feelings by switching off his emotions whenever he pleases.

I detected *something* in his eyes for me.

I can be wrong once but not always. It hurts me that he feels something for me and chooses not to do anything about it.

It seems so easy for him to make such a decision. Whereas for me, it's becoming difficult to be around him and it's just the first day.

His jaw tightens at my retreat but he remains silent. Obviously.

"Where were you going?" he asks after a second.

"I couldn't find anyone so I was just going back to the reception area." I add then, "*Sir.*"

"You can call me by my name, Rochelle." He speaks through clenched teeth.

"It is frowned upon for an intern to call her boss by his name, sir." I give him a small smile when all I feel is hurt and anger.

"I don't like you calling me sir." He says, then adds, "Not with that tone." Under his breath but I am not quite sure. I shrug off the last part.

"Mr. Will it is then."

He opens his mouth as if to say something but decides against it.

"About the staff. They're in the conference room. I asked my assistant, Olivia to gather everyone there. I wanted to introduce you to them."

Oh.

I nod and he starts toward one of the hallways, expecting me to follow. I do.

The office décor is classic. All in white and gray colors. Along with some greens and dark wood accents.

I almost run into his back when he stops abruptly in front of a door.

He holds the door open and moves his body out of the way for me to pass.

His action shouldn't affect me this much, but a simple gesture of him holding the door open does things to me I can't decipher.

As soon as I step inside, all eyes are on me.

Eight people are occupying the seat around the huge black glass conference table.

The urge to wring my hands overwhelms me.

My feet feel heavy like they have turned into logs of wood. I remain immobile for a few heartbeats.

My breathing turns shallow. I hug the purse I was carrying over my shoulder to my chest to cover the rapid rise and fall of my chest.

My eyes meet one of the women with raven hair. Her gaze squints as she regards me, her lips are turned slightly downward. I gulp and take a step back.

I'm taking another step backward when a warm palm settles on my lower back.

I look up and find Alan. He gives me a small nod and I find myself slowly nodding back as if we just had a silent conversation.

He takes his eyes off mine. "We have a new addition to our team. Please welcome Ms. Rochelle Moore. She is going to start interning for our upcoming property hunt."

After we are seated, he then introduces me to the team.

I learn that his team consists of people belonging to different fields.

The acquisition he came here for is getting delayed, so he decided to make a core team. To start looking for a new prospect.

The core team consists of talented individuals from various occupations.

Brian is an architect, Fin is a financial advisor, two females are analysts, and the others are appointed to look over his other hotel branches all over the world.

I finally learn the name of the woman who was studying me with a grimace earlier. Olivia Turner. She also happens to be his secretary, who has moved to New York from London to assist him.

After the introductions are done, he starts appointing tasks to them and I just sit there tongue-tied.

The realization that I am sitting amongst accomplished people makes me sweaty with pressure. But I am grateful for the chance.

"Rochelle, after filling out the necessary paperwork, you will be shadowing Olivia until further notice."

I immediately look in her direction and find her already staring at me. She gives me a tight-lipped smile and I return it before peering at Alan.

"Yes, Mr. Will." I nod at him.

His eyes darken at that. There's a tick at his jaw. "Great. Then get back to work everyone."

Finishing up the paperwork took about a couple of hours. As soon as I was done with it, I approached Olivia's desk that's stationed apart from the cubicles.

Apart from me, two women from the analyst department and some others are acquiring the cubicles.

The rest of the people like Brian and Finn, who play an important role in the team have their own offices.

The first task Olivia assigned me was to learn everything there is to know about the Will's Valley empire.

She handed me a few brochures and emailed me files relating to the history of the WV Hotels.

She also handed me a tablet. Even though my cubicle had a desktop computer, she asked me to use the tablet for work. She had said my role doesn't require a machine yet.

I wouldn't lie, the idea of knowing more about the enigma, that is Alan Will was tempting.

I decide to go with the brochure of London's branch first.

The picture of the hotel is something out of a fairytale.

It is a blend of age-old artistical structure like a royal palace and modern sophistication.

I gasp at the words written below the picture.

Will's Valley (London) featured in the Top Ten list of luxurious hotels in Europe.

I go through the pages, keeping a keen eye for any information about Alan. There's a brief mention of Alan Will being the owner of the Hotel and that's it.

The brochure mainly contained information about the services and facilities they provide along with the pictures of the interior.

I move to the tablet next. She emailed me various files which are named and sorted by the countries' names.

My eyes halt on one particular file.

Alan Will.

I quickly download the document and launch the reader app to open it.

Unlike previously, I read each and every word with rapt attention now.

According to the file, Alan's great grandfather started Will's Valley and since then, they have opened many branches all over the UK.

But it wasn't until Alan that they started expanding their branches across the globe.

It also states that Alan acquired his MBA degree from Oxford University.

He was capable enough to take the reins of the hotel group but instead started from the bottom and earned his way up the ladder.

At just twenty-five, Alan is successfully running his chain of hotels smoothly. And now he's all set to open another branch here.

I was curious as to which acquisition has him all worked up but I couldn't ask anyone.

I just know that the hotel he was going to buy and refurbish as Will's Valley is now unavailable. Hence, the property hunt.

The quiet space around me is suddenly filled with chatter and that's when I realize it's lunchtime.

"I expected you to be ready by now. Come on, I'm starving." At Olivia's voice, I look up and find her leaning against the cubicle to my right.

"Give me five minutes." Shannon, from the analyst department, says.

I stand. This is the time. I should talk to them.

This is the perfect time to start a conversation with them. My heart starts beating faster.

I rummage through my handbag and take out the lunch container.

"Hey, Shannon, Olivia…" As soon as I start, I lose my voice. Because Olivia turns her eyes sharply at me.

"It's Ms. Turner for you." She says and my face heats up with embarrassment. Shannon snorts.

"I-I am sorry, Ms. Turner," she cuts me off.

"Oh, please don't apologize, dear. It's just… only my friends can call me by my first name. But we'll get there." She gives me an encouraging smile before adding, "Right, Shannon?"

"Totally." Shannon nods with a smile.

I feel my spirits being lifted a bit.

I raise the container with a smile. "I made sandwiches, would you like to try?" I look at them with an eager expression.

"How sweet." Olivia gives me another pearly white smile. "Thank you so much for offering. I am sure they are delicious but we don't want to—"

"I packed extra, please don't hesitate." I extend my hand gripping the container.

Olivia's smile cracks a little and she leans away, wrinkling her nose.

"We already decided to eat at the grill that's around the block." Olivia swings on her heels and Shannon follows.

"O-okay." I give a small smile to their retreating back and slowly sit back down on my seat.

Unwanted pressure starts to build behind my lids.

With a few deep breaths, I overcome the feeling of sadness and grab my bag along with my lunch box to find a place to eat.

CHAPTER 8

Rochelle

"Good morning, Ms. Turner." I stand and hand her the coffee. It's exactly how she takes it.

I am early again. It's my third day and I guess today is the day I get to shadow Olivia. She has been giving me things to read until now.

It feels like I know almost everything about Will's Valley.

Day after tomorrow my college will begin. I'll be working only four hours a day.

Tomorrow, Alan will be heading to the first site from the finalized list with his team.

I need to start working with Olivia soon. We must co-ordinate so I won't come in the way tomorrow but can also observe everything.

"Morning." She takes the white cup from my hand and smiles at me.

She walks past me to her desk and I follow suit.

After she is settled, she looks up. "I have a lot to catch up on. There's no need to hover, dear."

Sometimes, no matter how hard I try, her words prick like thorns.

The words or insults are layered with her smiles and endearments. It took two nights of mulling over the things she had said throughout my working here to understand she was rude to me.

Earlier, I thought I was the one with faults. But I didn't do anything to make her dislike me. I can't even say that she hates me for slacking off when she has not assigned me anything past reading.

My suspicions of her disliking me proved to be true the moment I heard her speaking about me with Shannon yesterday.

I didn't mean to eavesdrop. But the mention of my name garnered my attention.

I couldn't help but listen to them discuss me in the break room.

Olivia despises me because she knows I landed the internship through my personal ties with Alan.

I don't know how she found out but it's apparent that she considers me worthless and that I am here purely because of nepotism.

Maybe that's why whenever I approach her to observe her work—because that's what Alan has assigned me to do—she gives me yet another file to read.

I want to prove my worth but how would I if she wouldn't give me a chance?

Somehow, she senses what I am thinking because she opens a drawer and pulls a thick black binder, and thrusts it in my direction, "Here."

I take it reluctantly.

"This contains stats of last year of the hotel. You are to study everything. I may question you about certain topics. So do not skip a thing, okay?" she levels me with a pointed look.

At my nod, she gives me a tight-lipped smile. "Great. Now…" she does a shooing gesture, dismissing me in yet another degrading manner.

"How about lunch then? Mr. Taylor, I'll be straightforward. You have been delaying our meeting when you were the one who approached me to sell the hotel in the first place." It's true.

Mr. Taylor, the owner of Hotel Paradise, personally flew to London and met me to discuss selling his failing hotel.

I was pleased with the offer as I was thinking about opening a new branch in New York.

There's no place for sentiments in business when it comes to me. I should've known such is not the case for everyone.

Because as soon as I landed here, a month ago, I started working on the project, simply assuming the deal is done.

When the day of his signing over the ownership of the hotel to me came, he bailed. And he has been delaying it ever since.

I did order my team to search for other prospects, but in reality, I had my eyes set on Hotel Paradise and it's quite difficult to let the deal go.

Hence, the phone call. Last-ditch effort to convince him.

But I lost my calm and maybe the chance of persuading him as well.

"I am an old man, Mr. Will. I am unwell and I'm afraid I can't make it. But it was good to hear from you." Judging by the sarcasm lacing his voice, I am sure he feels the complete opposite of the words he just spoke.

"How about tomo—" the line goes dead.

The old man just hung up on me. Unbelievable.

I toss the phone on the desk and lean back in my chair, shutting my eyes close.

I should've approached him with patience. But he has been testing it by avoiding my staff's calls. And my messages.

When he picked up the call today, I was hopeful.

I thought he might've made up his mind. Wishful thinking.

I don't understand one thing though. Why keep clinging to your hotel that is slowly dying a merciless death?

I'm offering him a prize no one in their right mind would.

I took his love and devotion for his hotel into consideration and decided to compensate him with the sum of money that would help him and his wife to spend the rest of their lives in luxury as they don't have any kids.

Where am I going wrong?

I stand and reach a hand in my trouser pocket.

Taking out the custom-made cigarette case, I stride out of the office.

I don't smoke regularly but when the stress hits, I need a drag to release the pent-up pressure in the white puff of cigarette smoke.

I am almost near the lift, can picture myself standing at the roof terrace in solitude with a filter-tipped Virginia blend cigarette hanging from my lips.

I quicken my footsteps but something provokes me to look to my right.

When I do, I stop in my tracks.

Sitting on the chair with a black binder in hand is Rochelle. The girl who is tormenting me by simply existing.

The reason I am this wound up is her. It has been five months since I've had sex.

I can blame it on the piling work for my abstinence. But I would be deluding myself, wouldn't I?

The reason I didn't or couldn't indulge in stress-relieving activity—sex—is because I can't get the thought of a certain *girl* out of my head.

She's wearing a black full sleeve turtleneck and plaid pencil skirt.

Her dark, silky locks are tied in a high ponytail. My fingers itch to pull the tie securing her hair.

I want to see her with her hair down again. I had a hard time concentrating on anything when she was sitting right next to me during that dinner.

That night, I couldn't get my fill. But now, I can watch her without any interruption.

I don't know what happened in the span of a few seconds because I feel calmness enveloping me by just looking at her.

The concerns that were troubling me are wholly dissipated.

Turning around, I start towards my office and pocket the cigarette case. No need for it now.

CHAPTER 9

Alan

Life has never been easy for me. Especially the growing up part.

I was barely fourteen when Dad passed away. Asher and I weren't close to our parents growing up so his passing didn't affect me much.

Mum and Dad weren't that involved in our lives. What they couldn't do, Asher did for me. He filled in their roles and was there for me growing up.

But one day even that bond came to an end when Asher left for Harvard. He left because he didn't want to get tangled in the family business. He left home to find himself.

I had accepted his decision but when his calls became less frequent, we grew apart.

I lost my hero. Not only that, I lost a piece of me.

I had to grow up overnight.

Mum directed all her expectations towards me.

I had two options. Either throw myself a pity party or man up and embrace what's been given to me.

So I started preparing myself to become number one because in the business world there's no place for those who come second.

Mum had tutors and trainers and whatnot to make me excel in every subject.

I graduated early and by twenty-three, I acquired my MBA degree.

I have a habit of winning. My mind's trained like that. If I set my eyes on something, I don't take a breather until I have attained it.

Yesterday, Rochelle's sight somehow calmed me but the bloody stress is returning with full force as I am going through the list of the lands and hotels that are in great locations but are facing a crisis.

"Brian, don't you think we should concentrate more on hotels rather than plots? Construction may take longer than renovating." I ask.

"I think we should explore both options. By getting the plot, we'll have more room for designing it however we want. Whereas rebuilding an already existing building limits us."

I nod, "What do you think, Fin, which investment is beneficial in the long run?"

"Mr. Will, the only way to answer it is by actually visiting the site. We should not leave anything out."

"Okay then, we'll leave in an hour—"

"Mr. Will." Olivia knocks on the opened door. "I need to speak with you."

"Give me a minute, Olivia." I address the men, "Did we cover all the points? Is there anything else you'd like to discuss?"

"No, Mr. Will, that's all for the meeting," Brian says standing up.

"Great, then make the necessary arrangements, I'll meet you in an hour at the reception area."

With a nod they leave and Olivia steps inside.

She takes the seat Brian just vacated.

Intertwining my fingers, I rest my elbows on the table. "What is it that couldn't wait another five minutes?" I frown at her.

Being my assistant, she knows full well not to disturb me when I am in a meeting. I would like to know about the pressing issue that couldn't wait another minute.

"I am s-sorry, Mr. Will, I didn't mean to." I wave her off.

"It's done now. What did you want to talk about?"

"It's about Rochelle."

Just the mention of her name warms my insides. What is it about this girl?

"Let's hear it."

"Are you planning on taking her to the sites with us?"

Her question baffles me. "Us? Olivia, you will be staying in the office and running it in my absence. And to answer your question, yes. Rochelle will be joining me, Fin, and Brian. Her internship is based on this project, no?"

"But she is useless." She almost whines. Which is so unlike her.

If she expects some sort of reaction, I give her none.

She squirms in her seat for a full minute before giving in and starts talking, "She knows nothing about operations we run here."

"That's why I asked you to mentor her."

"I tried, Mr. Will. But whenever I give her any task, she does it all wrong. In the past three days, I have realised she is more of a liability for us than an asset."

"Hmm." I trace my lower lip in contemplation. "Tell me about the tasks she failed in. Maybe we could find a pattern and assign her duties that are more compatible with her skills."

She averts her eyes and starts rubbing her neck. Beads of sweat coat her forehead in this air-conditioned room. "I-I don't want to waste your time by rehashing it. Trust me, she has been just slowing my work instead of being useful. We should let her go."

"Okay, go and fetch her. Let's settle this before I leave."

She gets to her feet with renewed energy and leaves.

Rochelle

I am in an empty room, printing copies of the document Shannon asked me for.

Olivia surprised me today by assigning me tasks that involve assisting everyone.

I have been running errands since morning. It is still better than sitting idly and reading.

I am arranging the copies when Olivia enters.

"Mr. Will would like to have a word with you, Rochelle." She smiles, and for once it reaches her sky-color eyes. And her usually pale skin has a pink hue to it.

I ponder on her words. Why does Alan want to see me? He hardly looked at me since my first day of working here. Is it about the visit? Brian had told me to finish the remainder of the tasks in an hour.

Maybe he wants to talk to me before leaving. I know he was in a meeting with Brian and Fin.

"I'll be right there. I just have to deliver these to Shannon," she cuts me off with a palm.

"That can wait. Mr. Will cannot. Follow me." She turns and exits the room.

Abandoning the papers on the table, I follow her.

"Come in." The tenor of his voice is deep and velvety. I can never get enough of his British accent.

Alan is sitting on his throne. Yes, throne. He looks nothing short of a king sitting in the boss chair.

His jacket is missing, leaving him in a crisp white shirt and a vest. From the looks alone, I can tell the fabric would feel like dream to touch. I can only imagine the cost of it.

His long, elegant fingers are cradling his jaw, partially hiding his stubbled chin.

Finally, my eyes slide up to their destination, his eyes.

A shiver racks my body as I see them aimed already at me.

"Be seated, ladies." He says, finally acknowledging the presence of Olivia.

Olivia slides into the chair smoothly. She makes the simple act of sitting down so sophisticated whereas I am a trembling mess.

The reason behind my uneasiness is his eyes. I can feel them on me now.

"Rochelle, today is your fourth day I take it?" I lift my head at his question. But it hasn't registered yet. Because I am still stuck at 'Rochelle'.

I love my name on his lips. I want to hear it on loop. Like I do in my dreams.

When he repeats my name, my lips curl a bit around the corners. I think I just died and went to heaven.

"Rochelle?" Olivia hisses and brings me back to the present.

SINFUL LOVE

"Yes," I clear my throat, my face warming up. "Yes, it is my fourth day."

Alan's eyes are amused as he nods. Like he's aware of the effect he has on me. Fantastic. I want to jump out the window from embarrassment.

"Can you give me a rundown of what you have gathered or learned about the upcoming project so far?" he asks in all seriousness. The amusement I saw in his eyes is now ancient history.

"I-I..." I look at Olivia but she ignores my presence.

What do I tell him? All I did was read. If he asks anything about his other branches, I can answer them promptly.

But he is asking me about the current branch he is working on. And I don't have a single clue about it.

"Let's change the question, shall we?" he asks calmly. "Do you know what type of goal I have in mind for this branch? I am sure Olivia might have explained it to you." No, she didn't.

When I still fail to form a sentence, he says, "Olivia, you were right. This isn't working."

My stomach drops. What isn't working?

"I told you so," Olivia says.

I can't comprehend what they are discussing about and it's making me nervous.

"Rochelle, I assigned you to shadow Olivia." I nod slowly. "But seeing as this arrangement has been proved fruitless. There's only one option left."

This is it. I am being dismissed.

I look down at my folded hands in my lap instead.

"Rochelle," he doesn't speak further until I lift my eyes. "This day forward, you'll be shadowing *me*."

CHAPTER 10

Rochelle

"This is pure bliss." I hear Emily say. We are currently lying on Emily's bed with sheet masks on, grooving to pop music.

"Couldn't agree more."

We lie there in silence and when the fifteen minutes are up, the timer goes off. I reach the phone and tap on the screen before removing the mask.

Judging by the light snoring, Emily has fallen asleep.

I shake my head and proceed to remove her mask. The process wakes her.

"Enough skincare for tonight. You seem tired. Go back to sleep." I move to get off the bed but she clasps my hand.

"I am awake now. Let's watch a movie." Her brows jump up, her lips stretching on a grin of delight but I see the tiredness in her eyes.

"You must sleep now, Em. It's getting late."

She shakes her head. "I don't wanna. Please, one movie. Pretty please!!!"

I sigh. "Okay. I'll get the snacks and you get my blankets."

"YAAS!" she jumps off the bed with bursting energy and I chuckle. She was fast asleep not one minute ago.

After I have arranged the blankets on the rug to my liking, I settle on it.

Emily takes her usual place on the couch and we start going through the options.

We are still at it ten minutes later. Emily groans. "It always takes us longer to choose a movie than it would take it to watch the thing!"

"Never has a truer word been spoken, sister." I laugh.

"Ahh, screw it. Let's talk instead." She shifts her body to the edge of the couch and glances down at me.

I turn to lie on my side to face her. "Sure. What do you wanna talk about? Asher?" I smirk at her.

Her face goes red and she hits me with a soft pillow. "Don't tease me!"

"Why not? You always end up talking about him with a dreamy look." I point at her face. "Like that."

She hits me again. "I do NOT."

I cover my face with a hand, laughing. "Layah," I try to say 'liar' in an English accent.

She gasps and gives me a stink eye, but her burst of sudden laughter betrays her stoic face.

"Oh my god," she holds her sides, still chortling.

"Jokes apart. I really wanted to talk to you. How's your internship going? Made any friends, kiddo?"

My smile dies, but I force my features to stay brightened. "I did."

"Great! And how's the property hunting going?"

The question stirs the memory from this afternoon when I went to visit a site with Alan and the team.

"The value of this land falls under our budget," Brian comments as we take in the vast expanse of the greenery.

"But we should think about the expense we may incur in building the hotel from scratch. As I've said before, it is a big investment. And if not done correctly we may face consequences." Fin advises.

Alan remains unspeaking as his eyes rove over the land.

"Let us at least take a good look around before coming to any conclusion," Brian suggests and at Alan's confirming nod we all disperse.

Brian and a hired photographer head in one direction, while Fin accompanies Alan and me in another.

As we walk, my arm brushes against his, igniting sparks within me.

Ignoring the demands of my heart to stay rooted at his side, I take hasty steps to put some distance between us, wobbling a little as the ground is wet due to a light shower from earlier.

I hear the two men conversing behind me and I take the time to soak the beauty of nature.

The air is cool against my face and I breathe in the faint scent of grass and wildflower.

Just then, a gust of wind tosses my ponytail every which way.

I try taming it as I continue the stroll but a fresh soft wind plays with my hair again, covering my vision with ribbons of my dark hair. At the same time, my heel gets stuck in a patch of mud.

Yelping, I lose my footing. My arms flail as I sought to avoid falling face-first on the ground.

My eyes widen in panic. The ground is appearing nearer when in reality I am hurtling down.

But before anything could happen, an arm curls around my middle and breaks my fall.

I straighten but my nails dig into the arm holding me as I focus on taking hard, labored breaths.

"You're okay." I look up then. Those are the same words he had uttered when we first met.

Alan is towering over me with an arm banding around my stomach. Why do we always end up like this is anyone's guess.

I try to step away but he doesn't let up his hold on me.

He turns me so that I am facing him, still captured in his embrace.

"Why can't you watch where you're going, Rochelle?" his angered tone startles me.

"Excuse me?" I raise my eyebrows in shock. Why is he *mad?*

"You could've gotten hurt." His eyes rake over me, the concern etched on his face making my heart flutter.

But then his eyes harden. "Stop being an irresponsible kid." He gives me a little shake, causing my body to crash into him.

A kid? So this is what he thinks of me?

My heart beats for him, sings for him, hell, even lives for the moments it can capture his little glimpses and all this while I was nothing but a troublesome teen for him. A kid. An irresponsible one at that.

My heart turns bitter. I had feelings for this man.

The harder I attempted to bury them, the more they grew. No matter how much I tried to suppress them, it kept surfacing.

Hopeless tears burn my lids.

A gasp tears through my throat when an unmistakable bulge presses against my belly. I grit my teeth.

The evidence of his desire is trapped between our bodies. Thick and pulsing.

I may be young but at least I am not a hypocrite.

"Kid, huh?" I twist my hips a little, purposely brushing against his erection to make a point.

Functioning purely on anger, I did something so drastic I know it would come to haunt me after this day, but right now, I have lost all my inhibitions.

Meeting his eyes head-on, I tilt my chin. I don't speak a word, letting my actions do the talking.

With a clenched jaw, he releases me.

Snap, snap!

"You just zoned out, Ro. What were you thinking about?" Emily asks.

I shake my head. "There's this new Netflix show we have yet to watch. It's about—"

"Why didn't you tell me before?" just like that, she's distracted.

I am half-asleep when the phone rings.

I squint at the nightstand clock. Who's calling in the middle of the night?

Grabbing the phone, I check it with narrowed eyes, sleep making them heavy.

Alan.

I sit up. Why is Alan Will calling me in the middle of the night? Is it to reprimand me about the way I behaved with him this afternoon?

I shouldn't have taunted him like that although he *was* in the wrong.

My mind goes rampant, thinking of every possible reason behind his late-night call.

The ringing stops.

I am still staring at the screen with a puzzled mind when it startles me by ringing again.

It almost slips from my grasp. I tuck my hair behind my ear before answering. "Hello?"

"Why aren't you sleeping?" he asks, his tone regretful.

"What do you mean by that?" I ask, perplexed.

Despite his rude comment, my body squirms on the soft mattress upon hearing his voice.

"I wasn't expecting you to answer." I still.

He wasn't expecting me to answer. But rang me twice.

Alan is one confusing man. He can't just call me anytime and say things like that.

I am not sure if he is playing with my feelings on purpose or it is because he is a victim of his own unclear emotions.

"Why did you call, Mr. Will?" my voice is weak. I shut my eyes, tired of his mind games.

Carrying the weight of unrequited feelings for him has sucked all the energy from me.

With Emily, I was able to forget for a little while but now those emotions have come back with a vengeance and are crushing me under its unrelenting pressure.

"I called to apologize."

"About what?" I ask, my voice nothing but a whisper.

"You know…" his voice trails. It is quite shocking to hear him flustered. I can picture him spearing his fingers in his hair while pacing.

"I really don't." I lie back on the bed, holding the phone to my ear. I am certain he is feeling guilty that I—the eighteen-year-old kid— felt his erection.

I don't want to hear his apology. Because it will cement the fact that despite wanting me he doesn't want to be with me.

I sigh in defeat. "Look, Mr. Will—"

"I am sorry. I shouldn't have called you a kid."

Wait, what?

"You are sorry because you called me a kid?"

"Yes."

"That's it?"

"What do you mean 'that's it?'"

"I-I mean…"

He should know what I am talking about, right? Or am I overthinking it again? Wasn't he going to address the elephant in the room?

"Rochelle? Are you there?"

"Yes, I am here."

"I would like to apologize again. I am sorry," I cut him off.

I shake my head like a fool. "No, it's okay—"

"Let me finish. Don't be a bad girl." My jaw drops when his deep voice turns husky.

I sit up again and lean against the headboard, his voice sliding over my skin and heading south, hitting between my legs, shocking me further.

"Where was I? ah, yes. I am sorry. I truly am. But." There is a pregnant pause before he continues, "I am *not* sorry about the other thing."

I am throbbing down there. And it is such a foreign feeling, I feel like I'm about to pass out.

My breasts feel heavy under my camisole. I reach a hand up to my left breast to soothe the pain. A zap of electricity shoots through me when my fingertips connect my pebbled nipple.

What is happening to me?

I must have remained silent for a long time because he clears his throat. "I know your college starts tomorrow." His voice indicates he is no more the man who just worked black magic on my body with a single sentence.

Don't be a bad girl.

He's back to being his old closed-off self. He continues. "We have another site visit. Text me before your last class starts. I'll come to pick you up." He hangs up. Leaving me baffled and... wet.

What just happened?

CHAPTER 11

Alan

Have you ever wondered why we often crave the most forbidden thing? The rush of acquiring it becomes more enticing the moment we learn about it being off-limits.

It becomes unbearably tempting especially when the forbidden fruit is within your reach.

All you have to do is extend your hand and steal it. But you can't. It tests every last bit of your control.

Slowly but surely, it makes you blind with lust so strong you have no other alternative but to succumb to it.

That's what happened to me last night. My carefully placed illusion slipped and I let Rochelle in.

It all started with my rash decision of ringing her. I shouldn't have.

I dialed her number intending to apologise about everything. The whole kid thing and also about my erection. That was highly inappropriate on my part.

But what did I do? I crossed yet another line with her by confessing how I didn't give two fucks about her feeling my hard, aching cock rubbing against her belly.

I don't know what caused me to do that. It may be her sexy as fuck voice doused in sleep—groggy and husky—that made me lose my fucking mind.

I was already doing a piss poor job at concealing my yearnings for Rochelle but last night's phone call was the final nail in the coffin of my career in acting.

All these days, I had been fighting internal battles with myself.

I maintained a cool head around her and always shut her down whenever she tried peering into my soul.

But it was getting harder and harder.

I kept arguing with myself that she is eighteen. That means she is technically legal.

My mind latched onto the fact that made her a fair game but the logical part of me shook me to think straight.

But the desire-filled looks she gave me whenever we were together weren't helping either. The shy girl was laying it all in the open.

After tossing and turning most of the night, I have finally made up my mind.

I have to back off. What's done cannot be undone.

She is not the kind of girl who would entertain the idea of a fling. And I can't pursue her and bound her to me at such young age.

She has yet to see the world. I refuse to be her distraction on the path to success.

She has all the time in the world to date but right now her focus should be on school.

I quickly type a text to Rochelle as I sit in my tesla.

I am parked outside.

From today onwards, I'll have to be more distant.

That's why I am sitting inside the car instead of waiting outside like a gentleman should.

With time, she would move on. I am sure of it. I just have to give her a light shove.

Rochelle

I am climbing down the steps of the building when my phone buzzes. Delving into my jeans pocket, I take it out.

As soon as I read Alan's text, I start jogging until I am outside.

My breathing is heavy by the time I spot the sleek black car.

Is it his car? What if it isn't? should I call to confirm it's his?

My phone pings with an incoming text.

Get inside.

It is him. The tone of the message rubs me the wrong way but I shrug it off. Alan is a man of few words.

My feet move again and within a second, I am opening the passenger door.

I offer him a shy smile once I am settled inside.

He barely glances at me before pulling away smoothly from the curb.

We head east on Spring Street toward 6th Avenue.

Despite the car being spacious, I couldn't help but feel suffocated.

After last night, I expected a change in our dynamics but I wasn't expecting a change like *this*.

It feels like we have taken two steps back instead of moving forward.

Maybe something happened and it has soured his mood.

The silence between us is stifling so I decide to break the ice.

"Where are we going?"

He takes a right turn onto West Houston Street, keeping his eyes solely on the road.

I utilize his silence to study him. He is wearing another three-piece suit. All black. Like his current mood.

A tick of his jaw confirms my doubts. He is indeed mad.

I give a start when he speaks, "We are visiting an under-constructed building site. We received information that the owners are having a conflict and are considering to sell it." His voice is clipped, all businesslike.

I notice that while talking, he didn't even look at me.

Come to think of it, he hasn't glanced my way since I slipped inside the car.

I nod and turn my head toward the window with a frown.

We never talked outside of work but still, I can tell something is off. And I feel it has something to do with me.

If I had a doubt something was wrong, now I am certain. Alan has been avoiding me like plague.

As soon as we reached our destination, he paired me with Brian when I was supposed to shadow him.

Hours passed with me making rounds and taking notes whenever Brian instructed.

I, along with the team headed to the diner across the street for lunch.

When Alan was still MIA, my stomach plummeted.

Why is he behaving like this?

To top it all off, Olivia showed up.

She smirked in my direction—which was seriously grating on my nerves—before casually throwing the comment, "Alan and I will be in the meeting with the owners" in my direction.

When Brian suggested I should sit in the meeting she declined and was quite delighted to add, "Boss's orders."

With nothing to do, I excused myself to wander off.

The building's first three floors were completed and the team had occupied a room on the first floor.

Currently, I am sitting with my back leaned against the wall in a room on the second floor. Away from others.

I fold my arms around my knees, hugging them to my chest. I lay my temple against them and gaze out the open window.

It's close to six in the evening. I cannot wait for this day to be over.

Why is his aloof behavior getting to me like this?

I shut my eyes tight, refusing to let the tears escape. I trace the wrist, missing the feeling of my dainty bracelet.

Seems like I am never going to get it back along with my heart.

CHAPTER 12

Alan

My fingers curl, trapping Rochelle's bracelet under my fist.

Remorse filling me that it's not digging in my skin. Even her bracelet is soft like her.

My eyes are still glued to her face. She is sitting with the team members and having her lunch. Or more like picking at her salad.

In the last ten minutes of my standing here, she hasn't taken a single bite, her eyes constantly scanning the entrance area. Searching for my signs.

I am standing outside the opposite glass window to where she is sitting.

I purposely asked them to go on without me. She needed this distance. To erase me from her mind.

It's for the good. I know it is. Then why does my chest ache?

As if she could sense me, her eyes snap in my direction, but I manage to turn so that I am shielded with the brick wall where the glass ends.

I open the suit jacket and place the bracelet in the inside pocket before leaving.

"Olivia? What are you doing here?" I ask when I reach the site and see Olivia waiting there.

"Mr. Will, here's the analysis report." She extends the file and I frown.

"You could've emailed me. I didn't need the hard copy."

Her face reddens. Nowadays, Olivia has been acting strange.

I nod. "Anyway, thank you. You can head back to the office."

"Uh, can I attend the meeting with the owners?"

I just blink at her.

She continues, "One of the owners, Mr. Shaikh prefers to talk in Arabic. As you know, I can speak the language fluently, I could help in translating. This way, they can see we have come prepared."

She has a good point. I'll have to take Olivia instead of Rochelle. The party was open to discussion with only two members of our team.

"All right. You'll come with me. Inform the rest about the same."

I loosen the tie as I step inside the room on the ground floor where others were waiting. Olivia follows. Upon seeing us enter, Fin stands.

"How was the meeting?" Fin's face looks hopeful.

I stride past them to the sofa at the corner of the room and slump down on it.

"Well?" Brian prompts.

I sigh. "Let's just say they have a difference of opinion among themselves on selling the property." Three of them in total had different takes on how they wanted to do this.

Did I mention one of them was downright refusing to sell in the first place?

I can feel their puzzled glances. Olivia takes over then, briefing them about the meeting.

What a waste of time. Closing my eyes, I pinch the bridge of my nose.

After a few minutes of hearing their chat, I stand. The room goes silent.

I scan the faces and realise the one I grew fond of is missing. "Where's Rochelle?"

They look around as if just now taking notice of her absence.

I retrieve my cell phone and ring her.

"Oh, she excused herself right after your meeting had started," Brian says.

With one hand cradling the phone to my ear, I glare at him. "You trying to tell me she has been missing for an hour and a half and you didn't care to check up on her?" I ask in a stern tone.

I avert my gaze because Brian has gone deathly pale.

I grind my molars, my anger escalating when the phone keeps ringing and she doesn't answer.

"M-Mr. Will... I am sorry..." Brian starts and I take a deep breath.

They are my employees. I shouldn't lose my cool around them. That's not who I am. They shouldn't fear me.

I demand respect instead of blind obedience.

"I don't want an apology, Brian. Next time if you're given responsibility for a task or a subordinate, you must be alert and observant." I gentle my tone.

Even if the words are non-negotiable, I don't want him to feel reprimanded.

Rochelle deserves a good spanking for her reckless behaviour and I am tempted to deliver.

I try her phone again. "We are done for the day. Everybody may leave."

I slide my gaze to Fin. "Fin, drop Olivia on your way home." Not waiting for another second, I prowl out the room.

Her phone keeps ringing. "Answer your bloody phone, Rochelle," I growl.

After checking every room on the ground floor, I contemplate whether to head upstairs or call Emily.

Calling Emily would only result in the unwanted hullabaloo. Deciding to go with my instincts, I climb the stairs to the first floor.

I enter the first room and take in the marble floor.

The cool breeze from the glassless windows has dropped the room temperature.

I glance at the huge window again.

The sight angers me more. This under-construction site is unsafe and Rochelle might be in one of the rooms like this one.

The thought of Rochelle being in danger's reach tightens the muscles in my shoulders.

I charge out of the room and tear through the remainder of the rooms with lightning speed.

Agitation vibrates through my body as I repeat the in and out again and again.

As I am nearing the end of the hallway, I ring her one more time.

Just when I am about to enter another empty room my instincts sharpen, forcing me to turn. I do and glance at the room across the hall.

The door is ajar and the chill washes over me when I peek in.

A figure is lying on the floor. From the feminine, small frame it is clear the person passed out on the floor just beside a huge window is Rochelle.

Pushing the door open, I march toward her.

She startles from the resounding bang from the door crashing against the wall.

"Mr. Will?" She croaks. Gripping her elbow, I lift her rather forcibly. She stands on shaky legs.

"What the fuck are you doing here?" My voice is thunderous. The need to discipline her makes my palm twitch.

Her wide green gaze meets mine, her small body quaking with terror.

When she remains speechless, I give her body a shake.

"Don't make me repeat myself, Rochelle. You're already in trouble."

Her eyes widen even more. Her chest heaves with hard breathing, drawing my attention.

She tracks my eyes and catches me eying her chest.

She narrows her eyes and jerks away from my hold. "I wandered in here and must've fallen asleep. I apologize for the inconvenience."

"Inconvenience? Rochelle, do you know how much you had me worried? I searched the floors like a madman—"

"Why?" she asks calmly.

"Why what?"

"Why were you worried, Mr. Will? why do you care?" she takes a step forward.

I narrow my eyes. "You're my employee which means my responsibility. Of course, I care."

"When will you admit it, Alan?" She's calling me by my name. I don't know what to make of it. It calms me and unnerves me at the same time.

She is asking me something I am not prepared to answer. I care for Rochelle deeply but admitting it would open the doors to the possibilities I might regret later.

I vowed to never become her distraction and I intend to keep it.

With two more steps, she stands right in front of me. Uncaring that she is invading my personal space.

"I don't know what you're talking about," I speak with determination irrespective of what I am feeling.

She is unfazed. "I am going to make it easier for you. Even if doing so would cost me my self-respect." She says by going on her tip-toes and lightly pressing her lips over mine.

Rochelle

I have never been kissed in my life. Like any other girl, I had many scenarios in my mind regarding my first kiss.

Like the classic romance novels, I imagined it to be epic. My hero would claim my lips just before saying those three magical words.

I had different notions for first kisses. Always assumed the guy would be the one to do it, make the first move.

Never thought I would be the one initiating the kiss.

I keep my lips glued to his, my eyes screwed shut. He has gone completely still against me. This is the only way to express how much I want him.

My hands reach up to cradle his cheeks, loving the way his five o'clock shadow grazes my palms.

With a bold move, I tease his lips with a light sweep of my tongue.

When his lips remain sealed, the act of my bravery wavers.

What was I thinking? You can't force someone to like you back.

At this moment, I feel strongly envious of the ones who are lucky enough to experience love. To be able to bask in the light and warmth of someone's affection.

It slipped my mind that he is Asher's brother. And not to forget, my mentor.

Still, I wanted to gamble. I wanted to risk it all and know what it was like to kiss him. I'd give right about anything to feel his hands on me right now.

But we don't always get what we want in life.

My heart breaks when I loosen my grip on his jaw, my hands reluctant to let him go.

I keep my eyes closed as I slowly peel my lips off his. But before I could land from my tiptoed position, I am turned and crashed against a nearby wall.

"What—" I don't get the chance to complete as my yelp is swallowed by Alan's lips. His mouth slants against mine. My heart gallops.

My body tremors when his large hands grip my hips and pull my lower region against him. I gasp in his mouth when I feel his hardness. He takes the opportunity to thrust his tongue inside my mouth.

I get drunk on his taste, his masculine, woodsy scent ruling my senses, his dominant tongue licking and sucking mine, demanding to submit. And I do.

My hands glide in his silky hair, tugging at them while he makes love to my mouth. The feeling of his hard chest against my sensitive breasts is driving me insane.

Is this a dream? Is this how a first kiss should be? So consuming and hypnotic? Because that is exactly how I feel. Consumed and hypnotized by the way his soft, perfect lips feel.

I feel my panties getting wet and I squirm in his hold, wanting to get more closer to him.

My pussy starts throbbing when he bends to grip the underside of my knee, hiking it up and curling it around his lean hip.

The moment his hardness rubs between my legs, a loud moan tears free from my lips. Alan goes still against me.

Breaking the kiss, he untangles from me and steps back, leaving me dazed against the wall. I keep leaning against it while trying to draw in much-needed oxygen.

"Alan?" my voice is hoarse and small. His abrupt retreat is making me worry.

He finally let go and chose me.

Right?

He has finally revealed the fire within him that matches mine. The fire I have inside of me burns brighter only for him.

He is wearing a closed-off expression which makes it harder to get a read on him.

"I'm sorry." He speaks in a raspy voice without looking at me.

"You're sorry," I repeat his words stupidly, my heart thudding in my chest.

"I shouldn't have… it was a moment of weakness. It won't happen again."

I am grateful for the wall behind me. I would have crumpled down on the floor if not for the wall supporting me.

Swallowing hard, I try to straighten but my knees buckle. Alan is suddenly around me, helping me to stand upright.

I force my lips to curl into a semblance of a smile. "I'm sorry."

I am sorry for stepping beyond my boundaries. I am sorry for being an emotional mess right now. Last but not the least, I am sorry for falling in love with you.

I pull away from him. And gather my purse which is lying on the floor before leaving. As soon as I step out of the doorway, the tears break free.

CHAPTER 13

Alan

"Fuck," I punch the wall, welcoming the pain in my knuckles.

You're going to be the death of me, Rochelle.

She tested every bit of resolve I had. Hell, I almost took her against the wall.

Why does my self-restraint weaken around her? I royally fucked up today.

Earlier, it was easier to resist her. But now that I have a taste of her, how would I tame the beast in me from claiming her as mine?

This girl calls to me on a deeper level. I am screwed.

I take a deep breath to calm down and that's when I realise Rochelle has left. Alone. Shit, I let her leave when I was supposed to drive her home.

I stride out of the room and make a mad dash downstairs.

I catch her just outside the building. "Rochelle, wait."

She turns to face me but her eyes are fixated on the pavement. Her fingers are clutching the purse straps with a death grip.

"Come with me. I'll drop you home."

"I am going to take the subway but thanks—"

"This isn't up for discussion, Rochelle. I wasn't asking you."

She looks up all for one second before casting her eyes down again. She gives a weak nod. Her tongue peeks out to wet her red, swollen lips.

Swollen from my kisses.

I blow a harsh sigh before leading her to where I am parked and holding the passenger door open for her.

Once she is settled, I close the door and round the car to get in.

My gaze sweeps over to her and she shrinks down in the seat, facing away from me.

My bruised hand flexes on the gearshift. It's startling how much her disturbed state is affecting me.

I put the car in reverse. My mind goes over today's events as I ease into traffic.

Like the afternoon, this car ride is filled with silence. The only difference is, earlier it was purposeful on my part.

And now the silence is loaded with unspoken emotions, thick with tension rolling off us.

I pull in her building's driveway and kill the engine. As Rochelle reaches for the door without any word, I lock it.

"Rochelle," I start. My hand reaches out to touch her but I stop before it could connect her skin.

It's better if I keep my hands to myself. But I want to see her. To make sure she's okay. I want to talk to her.

What would you talk about, Alan? I am truly sorry, Rochelle for ravaging your mouth like a starved animal and then shrugging you off like you mean nothing.

I grimace. I am an arsehole.

"Please. Unlock the door." Her voice cracks at the end and I fight the need to take her in my arms.

Forgive me, Rochelle. I can't make it better.

Helpless, I reach the button and unlock the door. Letting her go. I watch her climb out and run inside.

It's for the best. I repeat it over and over again. But it does nothing to convince my heart.

With one last look at her apartment building, I pull away from the curb.

My eyes stray from the laptop screen. The phone rings for the third time in a row since I set foot in the office this morning.

I can't avoid her anymore. With a sigh, I answer. "I wasn't picking up for a reason. Couldn't it wait for an hour?" I didn't mean to snap but she brings the absolute worst in me.

"Is this a way to greet your mother?" Lydia Will admonishes.

Closing the laptop lid shut, I lean in my chair and close my eyes.

"I apologise. How are you, mum? Is everything all right in London?"

"Everything is well. I just wanted to talk to my son." And why is that so hard to believe?

Lydia Will is a businesswoman through and through.

She wasn't cut out to be a mother and she never tried to act like one either. There is definitely a motive behind this call.

And the sooner she gets on it the better. I am already pissed off.

Rochelle didn't show up at work. I have her class schedule and she is supposed to be here right now.

She doesn't have any excuses to avoid coming here. My money is on yesterday's kiss.

I'm the reason she is avoiding coming to the office.

But my sour mood doesn't justify me being rude to mum. She is a lot of things but I am the only one left in her corner. And I can't hurt her.

Her relationship with Asher is strained as is, she doesn't need me to act like a dickhead too.

"I heard you are facing trouble with your acquisition." As always, I was spot on about the motive. I can picture her sitting somewhere in her two-story countryside house with a glass of red wine.

I asked Olivia to keep her updated about our progress. Now I am regretting it.

She has retired but doesn't quit meddling in business. Sometimes her inputs are useful.

But most of the time she gets a rise out of me. Take now for instance.

"Alan, are you still there?" she questions.

"Regretfully, yes," I mutter under my breath.

"Do you want me to fly there?"

I already have enough on my plate. I don't need more stress.

"I appreciate your concerns. But I have it all handled here."

She huffs and launches in one of her success stories from the past. This is one of her favourite pastimes. She often tends to share her business success stories to prove a point that she's better than everyone else.

"Are you listening?"

"Yes," I am not at all listening but it doesn't hurt to agree with her.

A figure passes by my open office door and snags my attention. I sit upright.

"Mum, I have to cut this short. I have a meeting scheduled. Take care." We hang up and I push to my feet and make my way to the door.

So, I wasn't imagining it. It was indeed real. There she is. Rochelle.

I watch as she reaches her cubicle and lays her bag down before taking a seat. She starts setting her things.

My feet begin taking steps towards her and before I know it I am standing right in front of her desk.

Her eyes travel up. "Good morning, Mr. Will." she greets with a soft smile.

I don't respond to her greeting. I can't. I just stare at her silently.

I should be grateful that she is not acting weird around me. But this is much worse. Because although I am greeted with a smile, it is empty.

Her forest green eyes that used to shine with warmth are now vacant of emotions.

There are bags under her eyes. Like she has been crying. The thought of her crying because of me makes my chest hurt.

Rochelle's eyes slide left and I realise we have an audience. Two of the employees are sneaking glances my way.

"Rochelle. In my office."

The shuffling of steps behind me assures me that she is following.

Once inside, I round my desk and sit. Rochelle keeps standing and I ask her to be seated.

"I would like to apologise, Mr. Will." She begins. And I wonder if it is about yesterday. I am about to stop her when she adds, "I was informed that one of my classes was moved from tomorrow to this morning. I couldn't inform you as I was already running late."

Oh. That was unexpected.

"It's all right." *What a lame reply, Alan.*

"Should I return to my cubicle?" she asks, not quite meeting my eye. And I think we are in dire need of a conversation.

"Rochelle, I think we should talk about what happened yesterday."

"Sure. Let me bring my diary. I have all the notes I took from yesterday in it." She moves to stand but I stop her.

"You know what I am talking about."

"I don't. If it's about the mistake that happened yesterday, then we don't need to have this conversation." Her voice is tight but doesn't border on rudeness. She is speaking like a professional.

I give her a small nod. And she wastes no time in leaving my office.

I hope she gets over it soon.

CHAPTER 14

Alan

It has been two days since Rochelle kissed me. Two days since I kissed her back. Two days of blue balls and cold showers.

But you know what is fucking with my head the most? It's her changed behaviour towards me.

The girl who used to watch me like I was the only man present in the room, now hardly spares me a glance.

She is by no means acting resentful; on the contrary, she has been her kind self. Despite us being in the same vicinity, we are miles apart.

I can sense the distance between us growing at a rapid pace. And the fact is eating me from inside.

I was never the one to let my personal issues affect work. But ever since I moved here, I have been experiencing a lot of firsts.

Like now, I have turned into a grumpy boss who is snapping at everyone because he can't get a girl out of his head.

This can't go on forever, Alan. Time to get back to your usual self.

I nod to myself and enter the conference room fifteen minutes earlier. The meeting is supposed to start at two p.m. That's why I am shocked upon finding Rochelle already inside.

"Good morning," I say. She startles, her hand flying to her chest.

"Oh! Mr. Will. Morning." She gives me a practiced smile, her eyes meeting mine for all but two seconds before she averts them.

As she resumes her task, I take her in. Her smooth, pale skin is on display as she is wearing a pink sleeveless blouse with a black pencil skirt.

I move to sit at the head of the conference table, the position giving me a perfect view of her side profile. My eyes glide over her delicate features. Her small nose, her bee-stung lips.

I continue my perusal across the expanse of her graceful neck. Loving the way her ponytail lightly brushes the curve of her slender shoulder as she writes something on the notepad.

Fuck, Rochelle is so beautiful.

As if she heard me, her eyes lift and meet mine.

There's something unspoken behind those green orbs that are pulling me in. It makes me want to dive into the depth of them.

Her lips part just slightly. The movement draws my attention. Heat spreads through me as I watch her take in a shuddered breath.

My eyes travel back to her eyes, the air becoming thicker around us.

Something passes over her features and her entire body goes stiff.

She returns her eyes to the notepad like we didn't just have a moment.

Shortly after, everyone starts coming in and the meeting begins.

The meeting goes by in a blur. And not once did Rochelle look up from her notepad.

She kept her attention solely on the damn thing and I was stewing in my seat the entire time, willing her to look at me.

By the time meeting ends, I am ready to get the hell out of here. But that's not what I do.

I blame it on the tension that was brewing within me because the next thing that comes out of my mouth is shocking even for me.

"Ms. Moore."

Rochelle sits up so fast like she has been shocked by an electric wire. She meets my eyes for the first time since the meeting began.

Her green gaze is a mixture of shock and anxiousness.

"Was the meeting boring for your taste?" I can't help myself. I love it when her eyes widen but then they glimmer with anger.

Why do I like it so much?

"Absolutely not. Did I give you any indications for the same, Mr. Will?" she tilts her chin and my dick twitches.

"Your body language says it all. Are you sure you weren't dozing off?" There are collective snickers in the room at my question but I pay them no attention.

I am behaving like a jerk but any reaction from her is better than nothing at all.

Her cheeks are flushed red. "I wasn't."

"Very well, then let's test it, shall we?" I challenge her.

She clenches her delicate jaw but remains mute.

"I'll go easy on you. What's the sum amount of the gross revenue of our London branch?"

She reads something on her notepad before speaking. "The gross revenue is estimated at 24 million dollars."

"And what percentage have we finalised to utilise for this project?"

"We never discussed this point. Instead, you decided on using as little funds as possible to avoid unnecessary loss."

She is right. Fuck. The girl was not only paying attention to every detail but she was also taking notes for the same.

"I think we are done here." My jaw is clenched, angry at myself for dragging her into this unnecessary drama.

"I wasn't dozing off, Mr. Will." she gives me a tight-lipped smile and walks out.

After everyone leaves, I stand and close the door to the conference room, and lean against it. "What am I doing?"

Pushing past the smirking employees, I enter the bathroom, my chin trembling as I lock myself inside a stall.

No matter how hard I try to be strong, he always manages to penetrate the walls I have been building around my bruised heart.

Why is he hurting me like this?

When he rejected me after that kiss, I didn't blame him.

He wanted me but chose to reject me and I accepted his decision even if it was hard for me to understand his reasoning.

It has been two days since he labeled our kiss as "a moment of weakness". And even if I spent the two nights crying to sleep, I walked into the office with my head held high.

Ignoring him was impossible as I am to shadow him. I embraced the pain and was doing everything that was expected of me.

I didn't want to give him a chance to think a teenager is acting up because she is heartbroken.

But what he did in the conference room was uncalled for.

Not only did he insult my work ethic, but he is also the reason I have become a laughingstock.

I don't want to go out there. I plop down on the closed toilet with my head in my hands.

When I feel wetness on my cheeks, I wipe at it angrily. I know these tears are not just because of what happened out there just now.

I am hurting because it was Alan who said those things.

The man I gave my heart to. The man, who not only broke it into pieces but also walked all over it.

I only read that love hurts. Now I am experiencing it. And it sucks. Love is supposed to make you stronger. But all I feel is weak.

Broken.

Hopeless.

Despondent.

CHAPTER 15

Alan

"One more round," I say, adjusting my grip on the racquet.

Asher wipes his sweaty face with a towel. "Brother, surely you can see I am drenched in sweat from head to toe." I blink at him.

His white shirt is transparent and sticking to his skin.

"I feel this is enough workout for the day." He manages to speak between harsh breaths.

Keeping both of my feet on the service line to avoid foot fault, I bounce the ball.

The sound of the ball slapping on the court floor attracts Asher's attention.

"Oh, hell." He throws the towel behind him and takes position. I give him a nod before my racquet strikes.

I hit the ball over and over with all the frustration and pent-up energy that's been accumulating inside of me.

One week's worth of frustration to be exact. Frustration at both her and myself fuels to push me to my limits.

It has been seven days since the conference meeting.

I shouldn't have provoked Rochelle in front of everyone. Because she is punishing me now. She stopped giving me her practiced smile and greetings.

The whole purpose behind my acting like a jerk was to get her to look at me but it backfired. The reluctant glances stopped.

She hardly uses her sweet voice. She nods in answer nowadays. Speaking only when necessary.

And there's been no progress in our project. Nothing is going my way.

My muscles scream from exertion.

At one point, I stop and tear my muscle t-shirt off my body. And then, we are back at it again.

"I am dead!" he throws his racquet on the floor before collapsing beside it.

I shake my head and grab my towel, swiping at my abs before hanging it around my neck.

"Don't be a drama queen," I smirk, feeling somewhat sane after the intense workout.

"You're a ruthless bastard!" he rolls his towel before throwing it at me. I slide to the side.

"Charming." I grab the water bottle from my gym bag and take a swig.

"Are you going to tell me what's been bothering you?" *Thoughts of your girlfriend's little sister who happens to be my intern. Oh, did I mention she is eighteen? Are you going to give your brother some tips?*

Jokes apart, I am almost tempted to ask but I refrain from doing so. Asher has a big mouth.

I just look at him and he sighs before sitting up.

"Is it work-related?"

"Not really."

I wince when he starts giving me that mischievous look. "Girl trouble?" he wags his eyebrows and I roll my eyes.

"You can tell me." With newfound energy, he jumps up and approaches me, an excited bounce in his step.

"There's nothing to tell." It's just that I kissed Rochelle a few days ago like my life depended on it and now I can't think of anything other than grabbing her and doing it over and over again.

But again, I am not going to tell him that.

"You know you can come to me if you need any advice about girls, right?" he gives me his cocky smirk.

I take out my phone from the bag and open the phone's camera. Aiming it at him, I say, "Repeat that."

"I am an expert when it comes to ladies. I can give you a lesson or two about how to woo them. Never hesitate to ask your elder brother...." He frowns at me. "Wait a minute. Why are you recording this again?"

"To send it to Emily, of course."

He lunges for the phone but I am faster than him. "You need to work on your reflexes, Asher. Want me to give you a lesson or two about *that*?"

He scoffs. "All right. Send it. Emily would understand the context."

"You sure about that?" I smirk.

Asher's eyes widen as if an idea struck him. "Do it! I want you to. It's been two days since our last fight. I miss it." He has a dreamy look on his face.

At my perplexed expression, he breathes out a laugh. "It's our thing. You wouldn't understand."

He sobers up then, "I was serious. If you need to talk about anything. Just give me a call, okay? You'd be surprised how much help a simple conversation can be."

I nod. Thank you, brother. If only it were that simple.

Rochelle

"How's Dad?" I bring the phone closer to my face. I missed her kind eyes and affectionate smile.

"I am fit and fine as always, Ro." Dad appears on the screen. Or more like his flannel shirt.

"Dad, I can't see you." I laugh softly when mom chides him. I even miss their constant bickering.

He takes a seat beside her on the brown couch. "How's my princess? When are you coming home? I miss your Sunday desserts."

"Need I remind you that you, my dear are diabetic. Don't get any ideas."

"I'll bring sugar-free chocolate pudding the next time I come home."

"That's why you are my favorite daughter! Don't tell Emily." He winks, earning another bout of laughter from me.

I talk for some more before hanging up. The colleagues still didn't return. I glance at my wristwatch. Lunch break is almost over.

I am supposed to be in Alan's office.

As a shadow intern, I spend most of the working hours in his office, observing how he operates.

When he is busy, he often assigns me with variety of tasks. Unlike Olivia, he asks for my inputs from time to time.

I glance at his office and gasp. Alan is leaning against his office doorframe, looking straight at me.

How long has been standing there?

He has become more and more brazen with his staring.

Whenever I chance a glance at him, I find him staring at me. And the weird part is, he never takes his eyes off me even after getting caught. It's like he *wants* to get caught.

Like he wants me to be aware of his staring.

I break the eye contact like always and fiddle with my phone. I should go to his office but I might as well wait for the rest to arrive. It would buy me some time.

It is not that I don't trust him. I don't trust myself.

I already made a fool out of myself and although I swore not to be stupid again, seeing him daily doesn't help.

Feelings don't die overnight. You can't smother it with a pillow to erase its existence.

Only time can make them fade. All you can do is wait. Wait for your feelings to die for the person you love and suffer in the process.

I give a start when the phone in my hand goes off. Alan's name is flashing on the screen. My eyes fly in his direction.

He is no longer *leaning* against the doorframe. He is standing in a rigid posture. One hand tucked inside his pocket and the other cradling the phone to his ear.

"You are supposed to be in my office after the lunch break. And according to my Rolex, you are one minute late."

He becomes awfully rude when he is mad. I gather my iPad and diary.

"I am sorry—" he hangs up. I look back up to find him missing.

I don't waste a second. I stand and make my way to his office.

"Come in." His deep, commanding voice makes me shiver as I step inside.

SINFUL LOVE

Alan is standing near his desk, undoing his cuffs.

"Sit." He speaks again. But his eyes are focused on the sleeves of his shirt as he uncuffs and rolls them up to his elbows.

I sneak glances at his veiny arms.

I take a seat, trying hard not to gawk at how tight-fitted his gray waistcoat is. It is most definitely custom-made.

With the way his clothes hug his muscular body, I am sure he pays a fortune to a professional for his entire wardrobe.

I am still looking at his forearms when he flexes them. "My eyes are up here, Rochelle."

My head jerks up. His lips twitch at the corner. And he's calling me Rochelle instead of Ms. Moore.

I blink a couple of times before clearing my throat. He is way too near and suddenly it's hot in here.

I open my diary and place it on my lap so my eyes could have a distraction. I don't want to look at him.

I hear the telltale creak of his chair, indicating he is on the opposite side of the table.

I am oddly disappointed at the fact.

"Did you check with the realtors? Any updates?" I hear him ask.

"Yes. There are no promising properties in my opinion, but I still made a list. Do you want me to email it to you?" I keep my eyes down as I wait for his answer.

When an entire minute passes in silence, I look up. "Is there a problem, Mr. Will?"

"You tell me."

"What?"

"Why don't you look at me? Are you uncomfortable working under me? if so, please notify me."

"It's not that…" I gulp, my throat suddenly dry. What should I tell him? He is the best mentor and I am fortunate for this opportunity.

It's my fault that I fell in love with him.

"What is it, Rochelle? Tell me. I am ready to rectify any mistakes on my part."

I feel guilty.

I wring my hands helplessly. I don't know what to say.

He gets up abruptly and heads to the ceiling to floor window. "I think you should leave. I need some time alone."

I stand. But instead of leaving, I approach him.

I stop a few feet away from him. His body is taut, tension radiating off him and it's visible in his tight posture.

"I am sorry."

He turns upon hearing my voice, his dark eyes frighteningly hard.

"I don't need your apology." He seethes through clenched teeth.

I have never seen him this angry. Does he blame me?

He is the one who has caused this confusion. He doesn't get to be pissed at me. I am just behaving like the intern that I am. What else does he expect?

"There's no need to be upset with me." I cross my arms over my chest. Mostly to hide my trembling fingers.

I am getting angry now but I am nervous too.

Alan has that intimidating aura. You are bound to cower to him. But this is not fear that I am feeling.

Like him, I am frustrated too but I am not acting up like him. This needs to end now.

He storms toward me. With a stunned gasp, I take a few steps back.

Alan eats up the distance between us and clasps me by the shoulders, pulling me close, my front flushed against his body.

"What is it about you that makes me lose my goddamned mind?" his intense glare rakes over my face like I am a puzzle he is unable to solve.

"Let go." I push at his chest. I am trembling all over. And it is not because my body is sensing him as a danger. Quite the opposite.

Before I could do anything stupid again, I have to leave his office.

"I don't want to."

My eyes widen. I exhale a harsh breath. "I don't want you to have another 'moment of weakness', Alan. I won't let you disrespect me again." My chin trembles.

I start pushing at his chest again but it is futile. He doesn't budge an inch. I give a frustrated growl. "Let me go!" I shout and that's when Alan jumps to action.

He swings around taking me with him.

He slams me against the wall of glass, the impact making me gasp. "What are you doing?" I ask, catching my breath.

I didn't realize up until now how close he is. He is leaning into me, so much so, I can feel his breath against my lips. Our mouths are dangerously close, only a sinful inch apart.

"What I should've done a long time ago." His eyes trained on my lips, his intent clear. His hands span my waist, pulling me toward him.

My eyes flicker over his shoulder. "W-we can't. The door is wide open." I can't believe I am considering it.

He says I make him lose his mind. But in reality, he is always the one clouding my judgment. I can't ignore the pull I feel toward him.

The knowledge that anyone could walk in and find us in this position is thrilling and mind-numbing all at once.

My eyes turn hazy with need as I look up at him. "We shouldn't." my voice holds no weight.

His dark hooded eyes hold mine captive. "I know." I watch his broad chest rise with labored breath. "Do you want me to stop?" His fingers flex against my waist, his nose brushing over mine.

I turn my head, brushing my cheek against his. "I-I want…" my voice is so low I am not sure he hears it.

What *do* I want? If I ask my heart, it would answer without hesitation.

It's him. Alan Will.

I don't have the power to lie. I can't act to be strong at this moment. I can't deny myself of him.

He turns his head so that our lips are almost brushing.

"I…"

He doesn't wait for my answer. Without giving me a chance, he captures my mouth and kisses me.

I moan, my fingers digging in his waistcoat. His hand snakes up, holding my jaw in a firm grip as his tongue swoops in. I hesitantly try to return his dominant kiss.

I didn't forget his taste. Our first kiss starred in my dreams every night. I relived it over and over, tormenting myself. Thinking I would never experience it again.

I cling to his shoulders as he continues to devour me. I surrender to him. A groan rolls over his lips as he deepens the kiss.

He takes and takes and I give him my all happily. He slants his head in the other direction, kissing me thoroughly.

My lungs burn from the lack of oxygen but I keep going. I don't want this to end. The ache is sweet and I crave more.

My hand slides up, circling his nape. He nibbles on my lower lip and I gasp.

Alan breaks the kiss. "Did that hurt?" his hoarse voice makes my clit tingle.

I nod slowly. He leans closer and sucks my bottom lip, soothing the skin he ravaged.

"Better?" he grazes my lip with his thumb. I am sure my lips are swollen from what he did to them.

I lick my lips and meet his eyes. "Yes," I whisper. Sounds of footsteps capture our attention and my eyes widen.

Someone's coming. I push at his chest but he doesn't relent. Instead, he looks completely cool and collected whereas I am a panicked mess.

"Alan." I whisper-shout.

"Rochelle," he mimics my tone, his dark eyes amused. Seriously? He finds this situation funny?

"Someone's coming." I point the obvious.

"So?" he pulls me against him tighter.

"Are you fucking kidding me?" my brows furrow at his changed attitude.

One of his hands releases me and slaps my ass.

"Language." He glares and my mouth drops open.

"I-I am sorry." I stumble over my words. "We can get caught, Alan. Be serious. Let me go."

"What would I get in return?" I don't know what to make of this playful Alan but I don't have time.

If someone saw us like this, they'll ruin my reputation. And his.

"Anything." I blurt.

"Have dinner with me."

My heart flutters at his words. Did Alan Will just ask me out on a date?

CHAPTER 16

Rochelle

A small giggle escapes me, earning a side-eyed glance from a woman standing next to me in the subway.

Rolling the lips between my teeth, I try to tame my stupid grin.

I close my eyes and see it again. The images of Alan kissing me.

I reach up and touch my lips, reliving the way his finger traced it.

I left early from the usual time because ever since college started, I only work part-time now.

I have two and a half hours until our date. *A date*. I cover my mouth to smother another giggle.

It is a wonder how someone can make your whole day.

I know we have a lot to talk about. We also need to discuss where we stand but I can have this one day for myself.

I can worry later. Today, I want to rejoice in this feeling.

It feels like I am flying, my feet light like they are made of clouds.

My heart is singing a love song.

It might seem cheesy but now I understand what all the romance novels are about.

I used to read them and often wondered, are those things even real? How can a person light up your mood on a bad day?

But it's true. I never used to pay attention to the small things but now as I am exiting the subway and walking with the people, I am noticing even the slightest of things.

Like the couple to my right who are walking with their hands clasped. The little boy who's happily licking at his candy.

I have been through this route so many times now but it somehow feels new.

Everything seems new.

I have a bounce in my step, my ponytail swinging with every step.

As I am nearing my street, I see a woman walking a cute golden retriever.

My feet carry me in their direction. I reach out to pet the cutie and ask the owner, "May I?"

She smiles her consent and I crouch down to give some love to the furry baby.

Any other day, I might have just admired the puppy from afar as my social skills kind of sucks.

But today seems different. Or is it *me* who's different?

I am humming a tune as I open the door to my apartment. I know Emily isn't home. She had texted me earlier regarding her plans with Asher.

Dropping the keys in the bowl, I discard my jacket and purse on the lounge chair before throwing myself on the couch.

Fishing my phone out, I type Alan's name and click on his contact and open a new message thread.

Where are we going for dinner?

I hit send. He said to be ready at seven but didn't mention the destination. I have to know the place to dress accordingly.

I'll have to borrow something from Emily's wardrobe as mine contains casuals and work attires.

I never texted him before. I wanted to but I didn't know if I had the right to text him randomly and outside of work.

And look at me now... texting him about our dinner date. We are making progress.

I like it. A lot.

My phone buzzes in my hand.

You'll know when we get there, love.

I sit up abruptly, my eyes zooming on the last word. Am I his *love*?

After a few minutes of grinning and hugging the pillow to my chest, I type.

I need to decide what to wear. Please, tell me.

I bite my lip and wait for his message. He is quick this time.

My cheeks flame as I read his message.

I'd love to hear you say 'please' in person.

I hide my face with the same pillow I was hugging.

He didn't mean it like *that*, right? I shake my head, utterly embarrassed for just thinking about it in a sexual context.

But then, I imagine saying that to him in person. I shake my head again, my entire face and neck on fire.

My phone vibrates again in my grip and I take a long breath before bringing it to my eyes.

You look breathtaking in anything you wear. But you don't have to worry about it. I am sending you something. Expect the delivery in half an hour.

What is he talking about?

I type my response quickly and hit send.

Alan, please, you don't need to send anything.

It takes him about five minutes to reply. I am biting my nail as I read his response.

There's that word again.

He is avoiding the topic. Tactfully. But he is successful in making me flustered again. I fan my face before typing.

Be serious.

I wait. And then wait some more. Alan doesn't text. I am beginning to think I pissed him off when the phone starts ringing.

Why is my heart beating so fast? I answer, "Alan?"

"I can send you anything my heart desires, love. All you do is accept it and say 'thank you, Alan'."

"You can't do that, Alan," I say softly.

"You don't even know what it is." His voice is patient.

"I don't have to. I just want your time and I am getting it tonight. I don't need anything else."

He stays silent. I check the screen to make sure he's still on the line.

"You're... something else." His tone is filled with wonder.

"Does that mean you're going to cancel the delivery of whatever that is you're sending?"

"No," he says with so much finality, I can't help but laugh softly. This is a stubborn side of Alan I am seeing and it is somewhat... cute.

I sigh, giving in. "Okay."

After a beat, he says, "I can't wait for tonight."

"Me neither," I whisper and I hear his faint groan. Suddenly, the room turns hotter and I picture us devouring each other's mouths again.

He clears his throat. "We need to talk. A lot." I couldn't agree more.

"That we do, Mr. Will."

His voice is amused. "I'll see you at seven, Ms. Moore."

"See you then." I smile and we hang up.

I check the time on my phone. It's five p.m. now. I get up and head straight toward the bathroom.

In twenty minutes, I am done with my shower.

My hair smells like roses and my skin, soft like silk after shaving every inch of it.

I change into fresh yoga pants and a tank top and wait.

Exactly ten minutes later, right on time, there is a light knock at the door.

I pad across the living room and toward the door. I open it to find no one there. That's odd.

I shrug and move to close the door when something catches my eye.

Sitting on my doorstep is a huge white box with a purple ribbon tied across it.

I bend down and pick it before getting back inside. I lock the door and head straight for my bedroom.

I place the box carefully on the couch like it contains glassware. I grab the phone and quickly snap a few pictures of the box before opening it.

I want to remember our first date. These pictures would serve as a beautiful reminder of this day.

I tug the ribbon and lift the lid. "Oh my god." I can't hold in the amazement as I slowly lift the dress up.

I had a hunch he was sending me something to wear for tonight but I wasn't expecting the outfit to be so extravagant.

By the look and feel of the fabric of this off-the-shoulder plum color dress, I am certain it is insanely expensive. The thought is troubling.

Placing the dress with utmost care on the bed, I move on to the next item. The metallic gold strappy sandals. Alan has gone all out.

I don't even want to guess its price.

My phone chimes and I immediately pick it up.

Looking forward to seeing you in that dress.

A smile blooms on my face at his text.

I spend the next hour hyperventilating over the hair and makeup. Emily had taught me the basics so I go with it.

After applying the light makeup, I switch to blow drying my hair.

Although it's almost dry, I do it to make it more voluminous. I am leaving my hair down tonight. And I want to look my best. For him.

I put on the dress and am surprised how perfectly it fits.

Sitting on the edge of the bed, I put the shoes on.

I move to the mirror and instantly feel the sense of déjà vu.

It seems like yesterday when I was getting ready for dinner that Asher hosted.

I take myself in as my fingertips brush over the silky soft fabric of the dress.

Dark brown locks fall over my pale shoulders and breasts.

The plum color dress is highlighting my complexion. It is snug at the waist and flairs at the hips, ending just below my knees.

It's ten minutes to seven when there's a knock on the door.

Tentatively, I walk to the door and squint to look through the peephole.

I am stunned speechless when I find Alan in a crisp three-piece suit with a bouquet of red roses.

I notice with thundering heartbeats that he's wearing a different suit from this morning. The slightly wet hair serves as evidence that he's freshly showered.

I am still ogling him through the peephole when his gaze moves straight over it.

A small smile curls his sinful lips as he leans forward. "It's bad manners to keep your date waiting." He says, making my jaw drop. I straighten and with a deep breath to calm my nerves, I pull the door open.

The smile he was sporting a second ago vanishes when he takes me in.

His dark brown eyes travel down my body, making me blush.

"I've never seen someone as beautiful as you." He steps closer and bends down to place a soft chaste kiss on my cheek. I inhale his familiar scent laced with the intoxicating cologne.

Pulling away, he hands me the bouquet. "Thank you for saying that." I tuck an errant lock behind my ear as I welcome him in.

I am about to find a vase for the flowers when he grabs me gently by the elbow.

I look up at him questioningly.

"It wasn't an empty compliment. I meant every word."

My heart does that little backflip at his words.

Shyly, I nod and excuse myself and run toward the kitchen. Grabbing the vase from one of the cabinets, I set to work.

Alan keeps his eyes on me the entire time.

Even when I offer him a drink, he just shakes his head slightly and continues to watch me like everything I do, every mundane thing fascinates him.

I make quick work of grabbing the small clutch and shoving my phone, keys, and card in it.

"Let's go," I tell him and he nods.

He patiently waits for me to lock up and then leads me to his car with a hand at the small of my back.

He closes the door behind me and rounds the car.

Just the sight of him walking around the car in that charcoal suit has me gasping for air.

Never in my life did I imagine my first date to be like this.

I never thought my date would show up at my doorstep wearing a suit more expensive than my apartment.

And let's not forget the roses. I got roses on my first date. It feels like a dream. I am lucky that this is my reality.

Alan knows what he is doing. The thought that he has already done this before dampers my mood a bit.

Come on, Rochelle. Don't be ridiculous. He is with you now. What more could you ask for? You are going to spend time with the one your heart beats for. Just go with the flow and enjoy the ride.

"Where did you go?" he says softly, shaking me out of my reverie.

"Huh?" I turn to find him already buckled up in the driver's seat.

He reaches out and grazes my cheek.

The touch is so light like a feather, it evokes goosebumps on my skin. "What's going on in that pretty little head of yours?" he asks in a low voice.

"I am nervous." I lean into his touch.

"So am I." he returns.

"Really?"

"Mm-hmm. I have never done this before," he confesses. My brows crease.

At my lost expression, he chuckles, his hand moves down, and clasps mine in my lap.

"I've never dated before. Never had the time to and never thought I would…" his eyes lock on mine. "Until you."

My breath stutters at his admission.

"I don't know what this is or how we are going to do this. One thing I am sure about is that I care for you, Rochelle. Immensely. I want to explore this with you." He squeezes my fingers warmly.

Placing my other hand on our clasped ones, I say, "I'd like that."

"Great. Then let's do this." With one last squeeze, he lets my hand go and starts the engine.

CHAPTER 17

Rochelle

I had my suspicions that Alan was going to take me to a fancy place.

But I had no idea he had planned the dinner date at a rooftop restaurant.

I am grateful for the dress he had sent because judging by the hostess' outfit, I know this place is swanky and my dress fits the bill.

There are only a handful of people dining in the indoor lounge.

And although the indoor lounge looks stylish and sleek, nothing beats the panoramic view of the wrap-around terrace as the hostess leads us outside.

Just walking hand in hand with Alan here has me smiling like a fool.

All of a sudden, Alan stops, halting my walk.

He bends his head and whispers, "If this is what it takes to get you to smile like that, then be ready to dine here every night with me."

Covering my mouth with my hands, I giggle.

The hostess turns when she realizes we aren't following her. "This way, please."

Alan looks at me and says, "After you, ma'am."

"Thank you, sir." I tease back in his accent and he raises an eyebrow, a playful gleam in his eyes.

With a chuckle, I start forward only to come to an abrupt halt again. Alan almost runs into me. His hands drop to my shoulders.

"What happened?"

"Look." I point forward with wide eyes. Sitting two tables ahead is my sister, Emily with Asher.

She mustn't get wind of my date with Alan. I'll never hear the end of it.

She is protective of me. For her, I am her eighteen-year-old baby sister.

I don't want to know what she might think of me dating my boss. Let's not forget Alan is a year older than Emily and seven years my senior. She wouldn't see that he is technically young. No, she would focus on *my* age. She is a mother hen and could react possessively.

It is for the better that we keep this under wraps for now.

I swing swiftly on my heels. "We need to leave." Alan doesn't question me for a second. He gives me a nod and interlaces our fingers.

Turning around, he walks briskly with me in tow.

I was bummed to think our date ended even before it began but Alan had a surprise in store for me.

I promised you a cozy dinner and I am a man of my words. He said as he drove us to his penthouse.

Now, I am standing in his lavish penthouse which is quite similar to Asher's as his penthouse is two floors up in this very building.

"What would you like to eat?" Alan stands near the landline.

"How about Chinese?" I suggest.

"Works for me." He nods and rattles the order into the phone.

As far as I know, Alan moved into this apartment almost two months ago but by the looks of the expensive-looking paintings hanging on the walls and the antiques placed at every corner of this place show how much he pays attention to details.

With such little time, he managed to recruit new staff, got his office space up and running indicates how much precision he practices in his life.

I moved in with Emily two months ago but I still have a few boxes to unpack. This man expects perfection in everything he does.

At such young age, he is not only independent but he is also ruling his business empire successfully.

Rich men his age often ends up on tabloids with scandals and hook-up news.

But if one would google Alan, the only results that would show up are about his hotels and little to no information on his personal life.

"Let me give you a tour of the house." He extends his hand. I nod before placing my small hand in his large one.

His fingers curl around mine and I get that tickling feeling in my chest again.

He walks me through the massive five bedrooms with a spectacular view.

I am in awe of the cozy library beside his study.

By the time we finish the tour, our takeout is here.

We decide to eat in his den instead of the dining room in the kitchen.

He carries the plate and I take the takeout bags and set them on the coffee table.

I sit down on the rug in front of the coffee table instead of the huge L-shaped sofa, a habit of mine.

I flush when Alan regards me with that studying gaze.

He shocks me when he unbuttons his suit jacket and discards it along with the waistcoat and flops down on the rug beside me.

"Alan, you don't have to sit down—" he places a finger against my lips, silencing me.

"Shh. I am hungry. Let's eat." I smile against his finger and nod my head yes.

"You ordered a lot of food, Alan," I say as I start opening the containers.

It is like a small feast for five instead of two. From chicken fried rice to noodles to steamed dumplings. He even got some pastries for dessert.

He rolls his sleeves and grabs the chopsticks.

He takes the container with noodles and dives in but instead of taking the bite, he brings the chopsticks to my lips. "You're so tiny. Eat up."

When I keep looking at him with a dumbfounded expression, he sighs and says, "Open, Rochelle." And I do. I get weak when he uses that dominant tone.

"Mmm, this is really good," he comments after eating a mouthful and then feeds me the steamed dumpling.

I have to agree it is the best I have tasted to date.

I moan in delight. "Love the way the texture of the flour they used feels. Makes me want to hop on the internet and learn the recipe."

"You love cooking?"

"I live for it. I make a mean beef stew. One day, I'll cook for you." I grin at him.

"Are you a closet chef?"

My smile falters. I drop my gaze. "You can say that."

"Ever thought of pursuing a career in cooking?"

"You mentioned earlier about needing to talk. What did you want to discuss?" I avoid his gaze and take a small bite of the food.

"There's no denying our insane attraction towards each other. But we know little to nothing about each other. I would like to know more about you, the real you. What makes you tick, what are your hobbies, and things like that." He tucks a lock behind my ear.

"You'll have to tell me everything about you too then."

He erases the gap between us by shifting closer. "All you have to do is ask." He speaks, his voice gentle.

"Do you enjoy what you do? The family business, I mean." He picks up his chopsticks and feeds me.

"Yes. I am the best in what I do and I love being in control."

"Have you ever thought of doing something else?"

He takes a solid minute to answer. Like he never thought about it, the thought foreign to him.

"I was groomed to take over our family business. When Asher walked out at eighteen, I became the sole bearer of my mother's expectations. Do I hate Asher for choosing his heart's way? No. Did I feel abandoned? yes, but it had nothing to do with Will's Valley. It is a possibility that if I had been given a chance like Asher, I would have carved a different path for myself. But like I said, I don't feel caged by my occupation."

"So, you have no regrets?"

"None." His lips curl into a semblance of a smile.

I move closer and rest my head on his shoulder. "I always wanted to attend culinary school."

"Who is stopping you?" He asks softly.

"Like your mother, my family has expectations of me. They want me to see where my sister is now. A business graduate, working in one of the biggest tech companies in the world." His shoulder stiffens.

"Did they force you into going to business school?"

I lift my head at that. "No, no. They would never force me into anything. I... I never told them about my dreams. I want to make them proud."

Taking hold of my chin between his thumb and forefinger, Alan tilts my face up. "You can still make them proud by doing what you love."

"It's not that simple," I whisper.

"Maybe we are the ones making it difficult?"

"You make it sound so easy."

"Because it is. All you need to do is tell them how you feel. I am sure they would understand.

Do not give up on your dreams so easily like it's nothing, Rochelle."

"What if I fail?"

"Then you'd walk ahead in life with zero regrets. At least you tried. Listen to me," He shifts so that he is facing me and grabs my shoulders. "you are dropping your weapons in defeat even before entering the battlefield. You'd be surprised by your inner strength. One of my rules is to never underestimate yourself."

I nod. Totally mesmerized by him.

No wonder he is one of the youngest Hotelier in the world.

This man doesn't chase success. Success chases him.

This charismatic man makes me believe I can do anything.

"You are going to talk to your parents. I am not asking you to do it right away. Take your time but you *will* talk to them."

When I keep looking at him in astonishment, he shakes me a little. "I need words."

"You're hot." I slap a hand over my mouth. I did not just say that.

A grin pulls on his ridiculously handsome face. "I'm hot, huh?"

"Please, delete that from your memory." I clasp my hands together in a praying gesture and he laughs loudly.

Not a smile or a grin. Full-blown laughter and it is the most beautiful sight I have ever seen. It makes me want to pause the moment and rewind it again and again.

"No chance. Now, tell me. Do you promise to talk to your family?" he gives me his no-nonsense look.

"Yes, I promise."

"Good," he says with a satisfied look.

After the meal, we move to the dessert.

"Can I ask you something work-related?" At his nod, I continue, "What were the complications you faced in the acquisition that forced you to change the whole project?"

He blows out a sigh. "The person who was supposed to sell me his hotel backed away at the last moment. Like he wasn't the one who approached me in the first place.

"I can't seem to get a read on him. His hotel is on the brink of ruins and I am offering a sweet deal."

"Why don't you do something that benefits you both?"

He tilts his head. "What do you mean?"

"Try thinking from the other person's perspective. What you are offering might not be enticing enough for him. Sometimes, money isn't the only solution."

He looks like he is contemplating my words. Still deep in thoughts, Alan eats a forkful of his chocolate pastry.

My gaze zeroes in on the corner of his lips.

"Alan,"

"Hmm?" he looks at me.

"There's something on your lips." I point with a finger, trying not to focus on how sexy he looks with his lower lip smeared in chocolate cream.

Taking a few tissues, he wipes his mouth.

"Now?" he shows me his face and I stifle a smile. He looks adorable.

He wiped most of it but the remnant remains on his lower lip.

Without thinking, I reach out with my hand and wipe it with the tips of my index and forefinger. There.

I shift my gaze up and catch his.

Time standstills and I can't pull my eyes away from his darker ones, my fingers still very much touching his soft lips.

His eyes get hooded and without breaking our eye contact, he tilts his head to kiss my fingers.

A zap of current passes through me as if being struck by lightning. I wrench my hand back and clear my throat.

If a simple touch can light my body up like fireworks, I don't know what will happen if we end up in bed.

CHAPTER 18

Rochelle

I read her text. Emily is staying at Asher's tonight. That means she is two floors up right now.

And I am currently sitting on Alan's couch. And we are about to watch a movie.

Neither of us was ready to call it a night and when he suggested watching a movie, I quickly agreed.

"You choose." He hands me the remote before sitting beside me.

"I am a sucker for romcoms," I warn.

"Hit me with your best shot, Ms. Moore." He raises a brow, challenging me.

Challenge accepted.

He casually throws his hand at the back of the couch and settles comfortably.

I browse through the list on Netflix, having every intention of finding the cheesiest movie.

I am still browsing when I feel it. The light brush of his fingers against my exposed shoulder.

My mind has never been so confused before. His touch is pulling me in like a moth to a flame but at the same time, I want to run the opposite way and hide.

I shiver when his fingers start drawing patterns against my skin, kindling a fire in their wake.

I squirm, pushing into his touch and also trying to escape it so he wouldn't burn me with those sinful touches.

Judging by his face he is completely unaware of how he is wreaking havoc on my senses. They seem more heightened, my body very aware of the sheer maleness beside me.

Alan notices my movements, his fingers coming to a stop. "You seem uncomfortable. Is everything okay?" he asks genuinely.

I shake my head, unable to form words.

"Rochelle, we must always communicate. We have to be honest with each other. That's the only way this could work." He motions between us.

"I find you intimidating. When I am near you, it feels like I am losing control. The feeling is oddly freeing. Like I am a bird flying but I also feel fear with it. Fear of losing my equilibrium and falling." I am rambling. I speak what I am feeling, trying to make him understand how powerful his hold is over me.

"I see." He removes his hand from the couch. Did I offend him?

I yelp when Alan holds me by the waist and lifts me. He arranges me so that I am straddling him on the couch.

"W-what," Alan is a mysterious man. I can never guess what's going on in that sharp mind of his.

Just when I thought I offended him, he shocked me.

He gathers my hands and places them over his hard chest and flattens his palm over them. "Now you're on top. You have complete control. Do I still intimidate you?"

I stare at him with parted lips.

Alan lets go of my hands, his arms lying on the couch motionless.

"I am at your mercy. Feel free to do anything to me. You get to set the pace. I'm all yours, baby."

This man. He disarms me with his sincere eyes.

Only Alan can make me weak in the knees and powerful like a queen all at once.

Right now, as I am peering down at this beautiful man, I want to choose to become strong.

So I choose to become brave. I choose to take what I want.

My hands sweep up his chest, to his broad shoulders.

One hand still clutching his shoulder, I lift my other hand higher, tracing the side of his neck, going up, up to his nape, and finally in his thick mane.

I massage his scalp and watch with satisfaction when his eyes fall shut.

Fueled by his reaction, I keep running my hand in his locks, loving the way it feels against my fingers.

A groan rolls over his lips. I want to taste it, his low groan. Want to feel the sounds he is making of pleasure against my lips, swallow it, and keep it buried inside of me.

When my other hand works a kink in his neck, he moans again and I find myself leaning down, covering his lips with mine.

He tenses slightly underneath me and his hands shoot up to hold my waist but stop mid-air.

True to his words, he is letting me set the pace. He's giving up, easing his hold on the control for *me*.

Our first two kisses were fast and hard, filled with passion and heat. Alan was the one dominating both of those kisses. Now it's my turn.

It's a boon and curse.

I loved submitting to him and now that he is letting me lead, I don't know how to do it.

Driven by my desire, I trace the seam of his lips with my inexperienced tongue.

"Rochelle," his low voice against my lips is pained as if it's taking a toll on him to remain still.

I keep showering his lips with small kisses and light licks.

"Don't tease me, love. You won't like the consequences." His hips thrust up gently.

The warning spoken on my lips and the hardness pressing between my thighs should be enough to make me run and hide but instead, it evokes something in me.

I want… no, I *crave* his touch. For the first time in my life, I don't feel skittish at the idea of being touched. I crave it, I crave Alan Will.

"Let me be the judge of it." I nibble on his lower lip, my hands close on his wrists. With shivering excitement, I slide his hands up to my waist, silently urging him to touch me.

He growls in my mouth, his fingers digging in my tiny waist, the sweet pain making me clench my thighs around him. "You're playing a dangerous game, baby." He kisses the corner of my mouth and bites down gently. He is still trying to control himself.

"I want to be reckless tonight. With you." His dark eyes glint and I go ahead and say something that would surely make him come undone. "Please," I whisper the last bit.

That snaps his last thread of control. He leans up and slams his mouth to mine.

I moan as our tongues come together, the ache between my legs growing and spreading with every second.

To soothe it, I press down on his hard-on.

His hands glide to my ass, pressing me down on him as he grinds his hips up.

Our mingled groans fill the air as we keep devouring each other's mouths.

My eyes roll back in my head when he sucks my lower lip in his mouth.

The sounds of our lips clashing in the silent penthouse is so illicit and dirty, it is making me flush all over.

Alan breaks the kiss and starts trailing hot kisses down my throat, his breathing heavy against my skin. "Touch me."

I *was* touching him. I look at him with dazed eyes.

Keeping his eyes locked on mine, he says. "Unbutton my shirt."

My breathing becomes shallow and my cheeks flame.

With shaky hands, I reach the first button but he clutches my hand.

"Remember, love. You never have to do something you are uncomfortable with."

He pulls at my heartstrings whenever he says something like this. He makes me fall for him even more.

I lean down and place a reverent kiss on his hand holding mine. "I want to." His grip loosens and I resume the task.

Alan brushes the hair from my face and kisses my brow, then my cheek, my jaw. "You're distracting me." I chide. Or try to because the words come out all breathy.

"Is it working?" he kisses the shell of my ear.

"You know it is." I move to the last button and the shirt falls open, revealing his washboard abs.

He leans against the couch, his neck craning to look at me and I swallow hard.

"You know what I want." His voice is thick.

I know.

I extend my hands and touch him. I trail them slowly down to his abs, tracing the groove of his six packs, the rise, and fall of his body, making it hotter to look at.

I lean down and place a kiss over his heart, his hand immediately in my hair.

Leaving feather-like kisses all over his muscles, I feel braver to lick one of his nipples.

He groans and tightens his fingers in my hair, pulling my face up for another scorching kiss.

Alan doesn't let up. He keeps kissing me, his hands controlling my hips over his hardness.

The direct contact of his bulge against my panties and his passionate kisses ignites a fire in the pit of my stomach.

Tension swirls in my lower belly and I squirm restlessly against it.

Breaking the kiss on a whimper, I throw my head back.

What's happening? My heart is roaring in my ears and I feel sweat trickling down my back.

Alan nibbles and kisses his way over to my collarbone and down.

The moment he bites the swell of my breast, my mouth opens on a silent cry as waves of pleasure wash over me.

Just when I think I am going to fall with the way my limbs are trembling, Alan pulls me to his chest.

We stay like this for what feels like an eternity. I think I have lost the ability to think or speak. I know what happened.

I came. I have read about it. I came just by grinding on him. The thought is so embarrassing, I want to dig a hole in the ground and hide in it forever.

If Alan realized it, he doesn't speak of it. His hands are trailing down my spine in a soothing gesture.

But instead of relaxing, I feel shy.

Untangling from him, I clear my throat. "I am thirsty." I climb off him and dash in the direction of the kitchen.

CHAPTER 19

Rochelle

One glass of chilled water does nothing to calm my nerves.

Oh, God. How am I going to face him? I am so mortified.

Gripping the marble counter, I try taking deep breaths. It doesn't work.

What would he be thinking of me?

I fan myself. The climax was so intense. That was my first ever orgasm. I am still sensitive down there.

My panties are damp and my heart, a quivering mess from our make-out session. Placing a hand over my heart, I try to calm it.

Awareness of being watched makes my skin tingle. My eyes lift to find him.

Alan is standing just a few feet away.

The way he is gripping the doorframe over his head with his shirt hanging open is so hot, I forget how to breathe.

He doesn't say anything, just keeps looking at me. I feel his lips moving but nothing registers.

"Huh?"

"It's getting late. I said I'll drop you home." He repeats.

Though his words are firm, I can see the unspoken request in his eyes.

Stay.

Am I ready to leave him and return to the empty walls of the home where I'll be all alone? Do I want to leave his side?

No matter how much abashed I am from earlier, I'm still not ready to part with him.

We are definitely not going by society's norms. What we are doing might be too much for a first date but I don't care. It feels right.

I know what I want to do. I take unhurried steps toward him.

It is at this moment that I know I can do anything for this man. I want to give him my all. Heart, body, and soul. And it is no teenage love. No.

I understand risks and I know this can fail at any time. Nothing comes with a permanent tag on it.

I am not a lovesick fool to think we are going to have a fairytale ending. Even if that's what I want, I know the chances of it being true are fifty-fifty. I am a realist and I know I am taking a gamble.

Because isn't it true? love is a gamble.

We fall in love not knowing what the consequences may be. So even if we end this tomorrow, I want to give him my all.

Why? you ask? Because I love this man and no matter what our future may bring us, I'll regret nothing.

His eyes take my every movement until I am standing in front of him.

Going on my tip-toes, I place a soft kiss on his mouth and say, "I want to stay with you tonight."

His hand leaves the doorframe and suddenly he is bending down and lifting me up in his arms bridal style.

I squeak, startled, my hands go around his neck. I fight the blush in my cheeks. "I can walk," I murmur.

He says nothing and starts walking. His stride is purposeful as he carries me to what I assume is his bedroom.

His silence is making me all hot and bothered.

Alan is carrying me with ease like I weigh nothing.

I cling to him as he navigates through the penthouse. He turns down a hallway and enters a darkened room.

Once inside, he lowers me to my feet.

He flips the switch, flooding the room with soft light.

My breathing picks up as his king-sized bed comes into view. The furniture is decorated in rich colors. Gold, and ivory.

Like the antiques in the living room, the master bedroom has a huge black vintage mirror. It's a contrast from the color scheme but somehow it is bringing the décor more elegance.

My gaze drops on the bed again. Am I really going to do this?

"Here." Alan hands me a shirt. "Change into this."

This wasn't exactly what I had in mind. I often read about first times in books and have seen enough movies to know the process of undressing isn't preplanned. It just happens.

But Alan is asking me to change. It seems so technical. So... unromantic.

Is this how it's supposed to be? Did the books and movies exaggerate the process of lovemaking?

"The ensuite bathroom is right behind you." He specifies, I try to read him but as usual, his face is blank of any expression.

I do as he says because he is the experienced one between us.

Locking myself in the ensuite, I quickly freshen up and get out of the dress and change into the shirt.

It reaches the middle of my thigh, covering all of my bits. I am still wearing my cotton bra and panties underneath but still, I am feeling very shy to go out there wearing his shirt.

I glance at my reflection in the mirror.

You can do this. It's Alan. *Your* Alan.

Nodding to myself, I turn the knob and step out. I stop in my tracks when I find Alan in bed. Naked.

Well, not naked. He still has his boxers on. I swallow, my throat dry like a Sahara desert.

"Come here." he pats on the bed beside him as soon as he spots me.

He pulls the duvet up enough for me to get under.

Gathering me into his arms, he spoons me from behind, the heat from his shirtless chest seeping through the thin shirt and warming me up.

As much as I am loving this, I don't understand what's going on.

"Alan…" I call out softly.

Draping his arm across my stomach he pulls me against him some more, snuggling into my neck. "Hmm." He speaks against my neck, the sensation ticklish.

"What are you doing?" It's a pathetic attempt to ask why he's not making love to me. Obviously, I am not going to ask him that directly.

"We are doing what most people do every night. We are going to close our eyes and sleep." I can feel his smile against my skin and can hear the amusement in his voice.

His behavior pisses me off a little.

"Sleep, sweetness." He kisses my nape and I melt.

"Goodnight," I mumble and close my eyes.

I could swear I wasn't sleepy a minute ago but somehow Alan's comforting embrace drugs me to sleep.

.

CHAPTER 20

Alan

Peaceful.

That's the only word that could describe how I am feeling right now. I don't remember the last time I was this relaxed. This content.

For the first time in years, my mind is at ease.

On any other night, I would be in my study with my laptop, working.

My thumb lightly grazes her stomach as I hear her snoring softly.

She fell asleep in my arms.

Tonight, I experienced a lot of firsts.

I am a man who doesn't like complications. Hence, I made a few rules and followed them religiously.

But ever since Rochelle stepped into my world, she not only bent them, but she also singlehandedly managed to break them into million pieces. The fact that she's lying in my bed is proof enough.

I respect ladies. They are a divine creation of God and I always made sure to leave them satisfied whenever I indulged in them.

As one of my rules, never once did I bring any lady in my house, let alone my bed.

Bringing Rochelle here felt right. I found myself opening up to her like I never had with anyone before.

It's no secret that I am a very private man. This is one of the reasons I have business associates and allies but not one friend except for Asher.

I'm grateful for this city. It gave me my first friend. I kiss the top of her head.

My lips curl when she rolls over and buries her face in my chest. She is so small. Her fragile frame makes me protective of her.

Mine.

The possessive thought surprises me. Is she mine?

SINFUL LOVE

Caressing her back, I can't help but recall how she threw her head back when she came.

I have never seen something so beautiful in my entire life. Her shyness heightens her allure.

She is innocent. It's obvious. This beautiful girl was willing to give me the most precious gift. Her virginity.

She trusts me so deeply and I want to show her that our relationship is real and doesn't limit to just physical attraction. It's true.

This young woman has bewitched me. I already feel attached to her. Sometimes, it takes a lifetime to build a bond, and sometimes, a day is enough.

In short, there's no rulebook when it comes to feelings. It can take shape and form for anyone at any time. You have no hold over it.

I hug her to myself and breathe in her scent. Roses. Just like her. I close my eyes and there it is.

Peace.

Softest set of lips stroke my throat. I groan, sleep fogging my brain. The silky caress stops and I go back to sleep.

A few minutes later it starts again but the torture is doubled when I feel movements against my dick.

Warm breath caresses my neck before the kisses change their course, traveling up to my jaw. I moan low, my cock waking up before me.

Another rub of that warm body and my cock hardens.

Disoriented, I try to open my eyes but could barely squint.

What time is it? Then I recall.

"Rochelle," My fingers dig into her hip to stop her wiggling against me.

She halts her movements. Good girl.

I am about to fall back asleep when I feel her plump lips on mine. My eyes snap open. Fingers gripping her hair, I tug her head back a little.

"Rochelle. No more mischief. Go to sleep." I reprimand. She might be feeling playful but I am a hot-blooded man in his prime.

I want to be a gentleman she deserves and I *am*... to an extent.

I want to court her, like old times. I want to take my time with her, knowing she is inexperienced but it's only so much I can do.

If she keeps this on, I am not sure I can hold it in.

Judging by the darkness through the large glass windows, it is still nighttime.

I kiss her forehead when she nods. She uses my bicep as a pillow and closes her eyes.

It doesn't last long. Maybe fifteen minutes because she is back at it again. Rubbing her stomach against my hard cock and kissing my neck.

Enough.

She gives a startled cry when I flip her so that her back hits the mattress.

"Rochelle," her name is a warning on my lips as I hover over her. "You're not a bad girl, are you?"

Her eyes are round as saucers as she shakes her head.

"Then why are you behaving like one?"

Her graceful throat bobs as she swallows. Her teeth sink into her full lower lip, drawing my attention.

With my fingers, I tug her chin, making her release the lip.

"What is it, Rochelle? I know you want to say something by the way you were trying to get my attention. Now that you have it, let's hear it."

"I want you." Her cheeks turn cherry red the moment she says it.

"You want me," I repeat. I am an arsehole for enjoying this but she is the one who's asking for it.

She doesn't understand. I am a demanding man. She shouldn't tempt me to the point where I have no option but to ravage her until she screams her throat hoarse.

"You already have me, baby." I dip my head and gently bite the same lip she was tormenting seconds ago.

"I want… more." she pleads with her eyes and although I know what she's hinting at, I am going to punish her by acting oblivious.

"More?" I raise an eyebrow.

She nods.

"What exactly does 'more' imply?"

I smirk when she huffs. Just when I think she couldn't surprise me, she goes a step ahead and shocks me by rising up and capturing my lips.

Breaking the contact she lies back, "This."

This girl is going to end me.

Her hand travels down my chest to my abs and before she could touch me there, I clutch her wrist and pin it beside her head. "Rochelle."

"Please, Alan." She raises her head and kisses the corner of my lips. Her free hand touches the centre of my chest.

"I'm beginning to think you are using that word just to make me bend to your wishes." I gather her other hand and pin it too.

"It's not working though, is it?" she pouts. I kiss it.

"You don't understand, Rochelle. If we do this, there's no going back. You'll be mine and mine alone. I have needs. Think you can keep up with my rigorous appetite?"

I am not kidding or saying these things to scare her. I want to take it slow and ease her into these things gradually but she has to know what she is getting into.

She gives me a heart-stopping smile. "Don't you get it, Alan? I want to be yours. I already feel like I belong to you. I want to be yours in every way. I want this."

She continues to slay me with her confession, "I have never wanted something like this ever in my entire life. I have never had sex before but I am not scared. I have never been more confident about something before—" I seal my lips to hers. Not allowing her to complete.

She is killing me with her honesty. She has a brave soul to ask for what she wants.

The way she opens her heart so freely for me to see her feelings renders me powerless.

She has severed every last thread of my control and all there is left inside of me is hunger.

A need so strong to claim her, I kiss her like a madman.

I thrust my tongue inside, devouring her. I angle my head to the side deepening the kiss, taking her mouth harder. I claim her lips as mine.

She is mine.

I get between her thighs, still devouring her mouth. My hands leave hers and she takes the liberty of running her hands over my chest.

Wrenching my mouth from hers, I peer down at her. For a moment, all I hear is the sound of our panting.

Silently, I reach for the shirt she's wearing and slide it up and over her head.

In a simple cotton bra and knickers, with her lips ruby red and swollen from my hard kiss, she looks sexier than sin.

Her nipples are hard as pebbles and her bra does nothing to hide them. I palm one breast and give it a light squeeze. She whimpers.

My eyes move up. "Tender?"

She nods slowly.

"Sensitive tits mean my girl is aroused." I flatten my chest over hers when she closes her eyes.

"Hiding from me already? I haven't even started, love." She gasps but doesn't open her eyes. I know just a trick.

I lean down and suck a nipple through her bra.

"Alan." Her green eyes fly open.

"That's right, baby. Take a look at what I am doing to you." I speak around her nipple, letting her feel the vibration of my tone.

My teeth take hold of her nipple, my eyes not leaving hers.

Rochelle buries her fingers in my hair, pulling and tugging. "Oh, God," she moans.

Making quick work of flicking the front clasp of her bra open, I get rid of the barrier. Her perky, full breasts spill out.

Her hands spring up to cover them. "Hands. Off."

"B-but…"

"Do you want me to stop?"

She shakes her head vigorously. "They are a part of you and hence, mine. Do not hide what's mine from me. Let me see them, baby."

Reluctantly, she takes her hands off.

My cock is painfully hard at the sight of her pink nipples. Her body trembles when I trace her areola.

My mouth waters to taste it. Bending my head, I flick the tip with my tongue before sucking it in my mouth.

Dropping open-mouth kisses all over her chest, I move to the other breast and give it the same treatment before returning to the first. I repeat it over and over again, torturing us both.

I am a big man. She needs to be ready to take me.

With a hand, I reach between us, skimming over her stomach and cupping her between her legs.

Caressing her over the cotton knickers, I trace the seam of her pussy with my fingertips.

"You're soaked, Rochelle. Tell me, are you wet for me?"

She screws her eyes shut. Her breasts inches away from my face as her chest rises with each harsh breath she takes.

"I asked you a question, baby." I slide her knickers to the side and part her pussy lips with my finger, the wetness immediately coating my digit.

"Y-yes," she breathes.

"Say it, I need to hear it," I order as I take one nipple and bite down, still palming her wet heat.

"I-I am w-wet for you..." Her face turns crimson.

Releasing her nipple on an audible pop, I praise her. "Good girl."

I place a quick kiss on her lips then move down, giving some love to her hard nipples which are glistening from my sucking, and glide down to her flat stomach.

I nip and suck my way south until I am face to face with her pussy. Grabbing the elastic of her knickers, I work them down her legs so nothing can obstruct my view.

I grip her thighs and spread them wide.

"You're fucking perfect, baby." I keep looking at her glistening arousal. It appears she has shaved everywhere.

"Alan…" I look up and find her perched on her elbows as she peers at me.

CHAPTER 21

Rochelle

I think I'm going to have a heart attack. The fiery gaze of Alan is enough for my body to catch fire.

The picture of him between my legs is so crude and wrong. I want to screw my eyes shut but at the same time, I want to keep looking.

The image of his broad shoulders between my quivering thighs is engraved on my soul.

He holds my gaze and places a kiss on my slit. A zap of electricity shoots down my spine. Holy shit. I don't curse often but this situation calls for it.

I try to close my thighs but his grip tightens. His breath on my sensitive folds is making me lightheaded.

"I am going to kiss your pussy." Oh, God. He didn't have to say that out loud.

"And you're going to keep your eyes on me the entire time."

"That's not fair."

"Who said anything about being fair?" His eyes darken with promise as his lips part and his tongue takes a long swipe of my folds.

My hips shoot up but with a hand on my lower belly, he flattens me on the bed with ease.

Losing momentum, I fall back on the bed and cry out when his tongue flicks my nub before sucking on it.

My heart hammers against my ribcage, threatening to jump out. I fist the bedsheets and screw my eyes shut.

"Uh-uh. It won't do. Eyes on me, love." I hear him say.

"Please, it's too much. I can't." Because it is. I can't handle the pleasure as well as the visual. It is just too much.

"Look at me or I stop."

I groan and with effort, I look down.

"Better." He smirks before resuming his torment. He alternates before sucking my pussy lips and licking.

The moment he presses his tongue at my entrance, I feel the tension simmering in my belly.

My head twists from side to side and just when I feel the release crashing over me, he inserts a finger in me. My inner walls cling to his digit as I clench around him repetitively.

When I come down from the high, I notice two things. First, that I am squeezing his head with my thighs and second, he is still licking at me, albeit gently.

"Alan… That was…"

"I know. You're almost ready for me." he inserts a finger inside of me again. Almost?

"I am big and to take me, you need to be fully ready."

What does that mean now? As if he could read my thoughts, he says, "Think you can give me two more orgasms before I fuck you?"

Wait, what?

Before I could say anything, his head disappears between my legs.

My throat is hoarse from crying out as he wrenches two more orgasms from me.

One from going down on me again and the second from finger-fucking me with his two thick fingers.

When I feel his thumb grazing my sensitive folds again, I jerk, "No more…" I don't think I can take any more pleasure.

He climbs up and kisses me hard and fast. "Do you still want to do this?" I know what he's referring to.

"Yes," I cup his jaw. He kisses my palm before climbing off me.

He quickly gets rid of his boxers and before I could see him properly, he returns and positions himself between my legs.

"This might hurt." He informs softly.

Balancing himself with one hand beside my head, he uses the other to run the head of his cock against my folds.

A shiver runs through me at the intimate contact.

"I love how you blush," he trails kisses at my cheekbone to my jaw, all the while he is rubbing his thick head against my sensitive folds again and again.

"Fuck, wait." He sits up and reaches across the bed to the nightstand and opens a drawer.

Retrieving a packet of what I am assuming is a condom, he closes it shut before sitting on his heels.

How can I be so careless? I forgot about protection. I am not even on birth control.

I watch with open fascination as he tears the foil open with his mouth and rolls it onto his shaft.

The movements are swift and practiced. And hot.

I try not to stare but it's impossible not to. My eyes jump back down and I gulp. Hard.

He is big. Not that I have seen a penis before, but that is certainly huge. This is going to hurt.

"I won't lie, it's going to hurt. But I will try my best to make it good for you." He promises as if he can read my fearful thoughts.

His bare chest covers me, my tits brushing his warm skin evoking goosebumps all over me.

My heart races when he presses the tip against my entrance.

"Alan…" My nervousness takes over and I start trembling. Why am I calling his name? I don't know, but it gets his attention.

Lowering his head, he bites on my nipple.

I cry out, my back arching from the bed.

My hands fly to his shoulders as he starts pressing inside. Despite my wetness, I feel discomfort.

It's hard even accepting his bulbous head in.

When I whimper, Alan stops. His mouth descends on mine and he spends the next few minutes kissing me thoroughly.

I kiss him back with the same passion, forgetting about everything else.

That's when his hips surge forward and he slams inside me in one hard plunge.

He swallows my screams, stilling to give me time to adjust to his girth.

Tears leak from the corner of my eyes and he breaks the kiss to wipe them away.

"I am sorry, baby." He kisses my eyes, nose, and mouth, apologizing through his affection.

The pain is there but not that prominent now.

I slide my hands down to clutch his sides. He shakes under my touch. It's clearly taking a toll on him to remain motionless.

Placing a kiss on his shoulder, I wiggle my hips a little.

"Don't move." He groans and rocks gently like he couldn't control himself. The motion stretches me and I whimper.

"Fuck, I told you not to move." His voice is low, hoarse. The tension in his body ripples against my palms.

"I am okay now," I reassure him.

He says nothing. Holding himself up with one arm, he reaches between us with the other to flick my clit. I moan helplessly as he keeps at it.

Then slowly, he starts rocking his hips.

My breath catches from the pleasure he is giving me from his touch and the fullness from his cock inside me.

I don't want him to stop. The pain, the sweet sensation, I want it all. My pussy throbs around him.

"You're so tight." He moans as he continues his gentle thrusts.

I clench around him again and he gives me his sexy, low moan once more. And it's my new favorite sound in the world.

My fingernails dig into his back, silently urging him not to hold back and he gets the hint.

He pulls back almost all the way out and rams inside me with a force that steals my breath away, the ever-present dull ache making this experience more exquisite.

Alan drives into my channel hard and fast until I am a blubbering mess.

SINFUL LOVE

Interlacing our fingers together, Alan brings my hands above my head as he fucks me like a possessed man.

Heat blooms on my cheeks. Not because of the sound of our mating that's resonating in his bedroom. Not because of how intimately we are joined. No. I am flushed because of the intensity in his eyes.

He doesn't say a thing but speaks a thousand words through his eyes.

The look in his eyes propels me to chase my release.

I shout his name over and over again when the orgasm hits me. I feel like my heart's going to explode by the way it's beating so fast.

The tensing of Alan's body is the only indication that he's close. He groans low as he lengthens inside me.

Alan fucks me with a few choppy thrusts before finding his release.

I lie there motionless for a few beats to catch my breath with Alan still inside me, his breathing warm against my lips and mine, erratic.

He then withdraws from me and pads in the direction of the bathroom.

I close my eyes, still gathering my thoughts and trying to get my bearings.

The bed dips again and I snap my lids open when I feel something warm between my legs.

I watch him in silence as he tends to my tender pussy. My cheeks flame when I see the white cloth splotched with red.

Blood.

My virginal blood.

After discarding the cloth, he gathers me in his arms, my back to his front.

"Are you all right, love?" he kisses the shell of my ear.

"I am." I'm more than all right. I am on cloud nine. I didn't think my first time would turn out to be this much enjoyable.

"Good. Now, get some rest. You need it."

CHAPTER 22

Rochelle

Just as I am exiting my creative writing class, someone taps my shoulder.

"Hey, you're Rochelle, right?" A tall blond guy asks. I am referring to him as blond because I don't know his name. I just know that we have this class together.

"Yes."

"I am Jacob," he introduces himself. I give him a polite smile. He returns it and just stares at me, his hand fumbling with the brace of his bag.

"Oh, I forgot, you left this inside." He hands me a cell phone.

I shake my head. "It isn't mine."

"Are you sure? Coz I found it where you were sitting." He frowns.

"Positive." I smile politely. I am about to leave when he calls my name again.

He gives me a sheepish smile before saying, "Actually, this is my phone. I just wanted a reason to talk to you."

Flustered like a deer caught in headlights, I stutter "I-I…"

"Can I have your number?" he gives me a boyish grin which is kind of cute but it does nothing to me.

I have already given my heart to a man. A man, who dropped me home this morning and didn't let me go until he kissed me breathless.

"I am sorry but I am seeing someone." I ease the blow by giving him a soft smile and leave.

In my eyes, I belong to Alan. And as far as my instincts go, Alan does care about me.

I'll have to talk to him about us being exclusive. Because I can never stomach the fact of Alan seeing any other woman now.

The classes went by in a blur. I'm not very proud to admit that I didn't hear a word spoken in all the four classes I attended today.

Every time I tried to focus, my mind roamed to last night.

Snippets of our time together had me daydreaming the entire time. I was even called out by one of my professors about it.

How would I concentrate on anything when I could still feel him inside me?

I wonder if he's thinking of me like I am of him? I am hoping that he is. He consumes my thoughts. Every single one of them.

Is it selfish of me to ask the same thing in return?

I can't wait to see him. I look at my outfit. Black tee and jeans and sneakers.

I still have enough time to go home and change into my work clothes and heels but I want to rush over to him now.

I am a goner. Shaking my head, I start toward my usual route to my apartment.

"He is busy. Your usual session with him is canceled. Why don't you assist me today?" Olivia asks.

My shoulder slumps. "Okay."

"Great. Get me my usual coffee and meet me in the brainstorming room, okay?" she doesn't wait for a response and struts off.

I can't even be pissed at Alan. He is a workaholic and I love that he is so dedicated but I can be a teeny tiny bit upset, right?

I was looking forward to our one on one session. Not because I was expecting some action. I just... missed him.

Regardless of the night we spent together and the kiss we shared this morning, I still miss him.

It feels like a decade has passed since I last saw him. I want to see him.

I couldn't even catch a glimpse as he is holed up in his office and now, I have to assist Olivia. Just what I needed.

With her coffee cup in hand, I walk down the hallway to the right where the brainstorming room is located.

My feet drag as the destination nears.

I had read a meme on the internet once about wasting a good outfit on an insignificant day and I can't help but relate to it so much right now.

I am wearing a white form-fitting full sleeve blouse. The *v* neckline is deep enough to show a hint of cleavage. I paired it with a tight red high-waisted pencil skirt.

The outfit is so sexy and stylish, I was giddy when I chose it to wear from my wardrobe but not so much now.

My head starts hurting so I loosen the ponytail a bit as my nude heels click on the floor.

I am almost there when a hand clamps around my elbow.

The travel coffee cup slips from my grasp. I don't even get the time to scream because I'm hauled inside a darkened room adjacent to the brainstorming room before I could blink.

I shriek but it's muffled by a hand on my mouth.

Before my eyes could adjust to the darkness, the door clicks shut and the large figure pushes me against it.

The push is enough to shake me out of my shock and I start struggling in their hold. I think about biting their hand but the familiar scent fills my nostrils and my movements halt.

The hand drowning my protests lowers.

"A-Alan?" I stutter as I suck in deep breaths. My heart almost gave out.

"Surprise." He whispers. With his hands planted against the door, he cages me.

Surprise?

Surprise?

"You scared me to death!" I swat his chest. He laughs.

"Don't laugh!" I swat him again.

He flattens my hand with his. "Enough." His voice is amused but firm.

"What are you doing here anyway?" I try to sound agitated but can't get much heat behind my words as I am happy with the turn of events.

He reaches beside the door and hits a switch. The warm light falls over us by the small circular ceiling lights.

"I missed you so I thought of stealing you." He missed me. My heart skips a beat.

Only he can say something like that with a serious tone and an impassive face and still manage to make it romantic.

"I missed you too." So much, I want to add but that would sound too clingy.

He bends so his lips are grazing my ear. The slight contact makes me dizzy with feels. So much feels.

"Liar." He pulls my earlobe between his teeth and gently nibbles on it. A shiver rolls down my spine and my knees almost buckle.

"I really did." I moan.

"Prove it." He kisses under my ear and I whimper.

"H-How?"

He pulls back a little and his stubble scrapes my cheek. The rough yet soothing sensation of it is too much. My eyes drift shut.

"Kiss me." he rasps in my ear. I twist my head and hide my face in his neck, suddenly shy.

The man has seen and loved every inch of my skin last night and still, his demand of a kiss is making my ears heat.

"I want you to show me how much you've yearned for my company like I have." Damn. This man knows how to ruin me.

I palm his cheeks and kiss him. Within two seconds Alan has taken over the kiss, his hands all over me. I don't know how long we kiss. Could be minutes or hours. All I know is, I don't want him to stop. I want him to keep kissing me.

I want to stop time and live in his passionate embrace but Alan seems to have other plans. He breaks away. "Have you eaten yet?"

What a bizarre question to ask right now.

"I'm not hungry." My brows furrow as I try to understand what he's getting at.

"But I am. Mind if I eat?"

O-kay. Guess a hot make-out session can work up your appetite.

Distractedly, I ask him to move so I could open the door. Feeling kind of bummed but what can I do? Alan makes me greedy for his touch.

Instead of stepping back, he stays put. "You didn't ask me what I want to eat." His dark chocolate eyes are hotter than before.

His words and eyes are confusing me.

Frowning, I ask, "What do you want to eat, Alan?" why is it sounding as if we are dirty talking?

My breath catches when he sinks to his knees in front of me. "You."

I can't believe my ears. Did he say he wants to eat... *me?*

"Don't keep me waiting, Rochelle. Lift your skirt." He is the one on his knees and I am the one who's feeling dominated.

My hands reach down at the hem of the skirt.

"Rochelle." His voice is low and deep like a warning. I quit playing with the skirt and start tugging it up. The whole time, Alan simply stares.

When the skirt is bunched up around my waist, I expect Alan to look at my panties instead of my face. Somehow, that is more torturous than having him staring at my panty-covered pussy.

"Relax, baby." His neck cranes to look at me. His hands finally touch me as he runs them up my bare thighs. I wonder if he can feel the tremors his mere touch is causing against his fingertips?

His hands move up until they are gripping my ass and jerks me toward him. At the same time, Alan leans forward and presses his nose between my legs.

He inhales deeply, breathing me in.

Oh my god...

The vision is so *wrong...* so *crass,* I have to close my eyes.

"You smell delicious... and mine." His lips move against my panties which are now sickeningly wet, sending tingles through my body. Heat blooms over my neck and travels up my cheeks.

Why is the room getting hotter?

I whimper when he licks me over the cotton barrier. He does it again but this time his tongue takes a long swipe. With the back of my hand, I suppress a moan.

"Alan... Olivia might be right next door. W-we shouldn't..." I open my eyes, my hand dropping to his shoulder. I am so turned on, I can't speak a full sentence without stuttering.

"Then you better be quiet. You don't want to get caught with me tongue-fucking you now, do you?" his dark blazing eyes meet mine. Any protests I have dies in my throat when he fists my panties and rips them off me.

He pushes my trembling legs open and studies my pussy which is soaking wet with arousal for him.

Without wasting a second, he dips his head between my legs. My eyes roll back in my head when he presses a kiss on my pussy.

That's where his gentleness ends as his grip on me tightens while he devours me. His mouth sucks on my still sore flesh, nibbling on the pussy lips before thrusting his tongue inside me.

Like a ragdoll, he arranges me by pulling one of my legs up and over his broad shoulder and starts eating me out with renewed hunger.

My fingers tug at his hair, confused between pulling him closer and pushing him away because the pleasure is too much. Almost unbearable.

The moment his lips catch my clit between them and give it a light nibble, I let go. My world shatters and explodes.

The need to keep the release going has my hips bucking against his tongue. I ride the wave as my hand keeps him in place.

Conscious not to make a sound, I bite my lower lip hard until I taste metal.

I sag against the door, disoriented by the intense orgasm he gave me. That was too much.

He is too much. But in a good way. Oh, God. My thoughts don't make sense. Might be because he sucked the sense out of me.

Alan stands and tugs me. I happily go to him, my face against his chest and his arms wrapped around me.

I hear his steady heartbeats. Unlike mine, his appears normal and controlled.

How does he do it?

He kisses my hair and I hug him more tightly. "Baby, aren't you supposed to be assisting Olivia?"

His question makes me pull my head back. "Why did you cancel our session?"

He places another kiss on my forehead and says, "Do you remember the advice you gave me last night. About how money isn't always the solution?"

Yes, about his acquisition. "Yeah."

"Well, I was struck by an idea when I was driving home after dropping you this morning. I have a feeling this might work in my favor."

I kiss his chest. "I believe in you." His eyes turn soft.

"Thank you. It's hard but I'll let you go for now."

"Shit. Olivia is probably going to kill me!" I turn and am about to open the door when his palm connects my bottom. I jump. Alan just spanked me.

I turn with a frown marring my brows, and find his firm gaze on me.

"Language, Rochelle."

"But…"

"No buts. And don't worry about Olivia, I gave her a task that would keep her busy for a while with Shanon."

"Why didn't you tell me that before?" I glare at him.

"The thought of someone catching you heightens the pleasure. The thrill of being caught made you so wet."

I avert my eyes.

"Please don't," I beg.

"I love your shyness, baby. I loved it even more when you let go of it and came all over my face." I cover his mouth to stop him from saying anything further.

He lowers my hand. "I want you in my bed. Tonight."

I nod even though he wasn't asking. He presses one last kiss to my lips before opening the door.

CHAPTER 23

Rochelle

"What are we doing here?" I ask him as Alan's new driver John, stops at a boutique on Madison Avenue.

"I've already told you." He climbs out and extends his hand for me to take. I place my hand in his and exit the car.

"You're trying to tell me we are here for a... business meeting?" I fix him with an incredulous stare.

When Alan told me we are heading for an important meeting, I certainly wasn't expecting it to be here.

He takes my hand and enters. The expensive-looking clothes around confuse me.

I stop Alan in his track by tightening my fingers around his.

"You do realize this is a ladies-only boutique, don't you?" I raise my brows.

"My vision is working perfectly fine, love." The corner of his mouth lifts.

When I still don't move, he leans down. His lips skim the shell of my ear. "You remember last night's punishment, don't you?"

His question brings a blush to my face as erotic pictures crash through my mind. How can I forget? He spanked my ass red. I knew Alan was intense but he gave that word a new meaning.

The day he went down on me in that empty office room three weeks ago, something changed between us.

We became insatiable when it came to sex. And reckless.

Last night, Alan was at my place. Now that Emily has moved in with Asher, we have been spending most of the nights together.

I was feeling bold so I tried to lead in bed by unbuckling his belt and taking him in my mouth. I didn't let up until he came down my throat. So as a punishment he spanked me. It hurt. So much so that I was whimpering every time the sheets grazed against the sensitive skin.

The punishment wasn't over. He kept me up all night by fucking me in every position possible until I passed out.

Taking advantage of my flustered state, Alan wraps his hand around my waist and walks us deeper into the store.

A salesgirl who seems to be older than me by a couple of years suddenly appears at our side.

"Well, hello! Welcome, how can I help you?" she asks Alan as she twirls a lock of her auburn hair, sporting a flirtatious smile.

I am a person who thinks twice before harming a fly, so why am I suddenly feeling very violent toward this girl?

"Hello. Can you lead us to the dress department? We want something for this beautiful young lady."

My eyes fly up. "What?"

She looks at me then, albeit reluctantly, her eyes trailing over my body from top to bottom. "What kind of dress do you have in mind? Evening gowns, midis?"

"What would you suggest for a friend's engagement party?"

Is he talking about Mason and Lucas's party? And why are they conversing like I am invisible?

"I am standing right here." I grit out.

"We have the latest collection that might suit the occasion. Please follow me," she tells him before turning on her heels.

Alan whisks me to the right, following the chatty salesgirl.

"Alan… I don't need a new dress."

This man. No matter what you do, he'll talk to you only when he thinks is necessary.

Right now, he is in the mood of ignoring me.

"Remember the dress you sent for our first date? I'll wear that for the party. I can't afford this." I wave a hand at the store, embarrassment coloring my cheeks.

"I am paying."

I shake my head vehemently but he places a finger on my lips. "I hate repeating myself but for you, I am going to say it again. Be it dresses or diamonds or countless orgasms, if I give you something, all you have to do is accept it and say 'Thank you, Alan.' Am I clear?"

When I say nothing, he squeezes my waist. "Yes, Sir," I grumble. He can be bossy sometimes.

Just because I am agreeing doesn't mean I have to like it.

"Are you trying to get punished? Is that it?" he asks, stealing the air from my lungs.

I try not to shiver. "I hate you," I whisper.

"Do you now?" his tone is mocking. Like he knows I don't mean a single word I just said.

No matter how much he bosses me around, I can never hate him. I love him like I breathe air.

It's natural and can't be helped. And I'll stop loving him when I would stop breathing.

The salesgirl starts plucking out pieces of my size and hands them to me.

I notice there's no price tag on a single piece she has handed me and that can only mean one thing. It is super expensive.

I shake my head. "Alan... no."

"Yes."

The salesgirl escorts me to a white fitting room.

With hesitation, I regard the accumulated dresses I am left alone with.

Sighing, I set to try them on one by one.

The first piece I go with is a High-neckline black short dress with long sleeves. The fitted velvet iridescent sequins and the open back is beautiful but not my style. It's too flashy and the last thing I want is to garner attention. Still, I walk out to show him.

He asks me to turn and I do. His face is impassive as he asks me to try another. I try on the next dress and his response doesn't change.

On the fourth dress, I understand his pattern. If the dress is too revealing, he orders to change.

Once inside again, I pick the satin slate blue number. After changing into the dress, I look into the dressing room mirror and blush.

I look… *sexy*.

The satin sheen falls from the skinny straps into a V-neck.

The tight skirt flaunts my curves. I like this one. This dress is by far the only one that shows less skin and gives off a sensual vibe.

With a smile, I go out and find Alan typing away on the phone.

I clear my throat and his eyes flit to where I am standing.

"I like this one. What do you think?"

His eyes scan me. My skin heats when his gaze lingers on my breast, then it trails to my curves before his eyes come up and lock on mine.

He curtly shakes his head.

"What's wrong with this dress?" My palms graze the soft fabric at my hips.

"Do as you're told, Rochelle." He glares.

"Don't I look good in it?" I frown.

He sighs. "You look beautiful, baby but I want you to try something else."

"Why can't I have this one?"

"Do not argue with me."

"Fine. Then I am not letting you buy me anything." I tilt my chin.

He looks at me for a beat too long and it's enough to make me squirm.

Alan tilts his head to the side. "You're going to defy me now?"

"I liked this one the best is all I am saying."

"Maybe I should take a look at the rest of the dresses."

He drags me back into the dressing room and closes the door behind us.

"Strip."

I open my mouth but he cuts me off.

"Defy me again and the people out there will know how you moan my name when I tan your arse red."

My breath hitches at his threat. I watch him with wide eyes, my head titled back as he towers over me.

He unbuttons his suit jacket and gets rid of it. He is not wearing a vest today which leaves him in a white shirt, blue silk tie, and trousers.

In the small room, he eats up most of the space.

The air is affected by his heady cologne. I feel my red satin thong going damp by his nearness.

There's been an upgrade in my underwear collection. I knew he found my cotton panties hot because he had told me so on many occasions but I bought a few sets of lingerie.

It makes me feel sexy.

He towers over me, cornering me against the mirrored wall.

He reaches for my ponytail and pulls the band from my hair.

I twist and kiss the corner of his mouth. "I really liked this dress. Please let me have it." I don't care that much about the dress.

I want to see whether he listens to me or not. I want to see if he values my wishes.

I kiss his clean-shaven jaw. Only because I can't resist him.

My upper arms are gripped and I am twisted so fast, I lose my breath.

Gathering my hair over my shoulder, Alan leans down and bites down on my neck. "If we are buying this skimpy piece of fabric you call a dress then I should christen it right here and now by fucking you in it."

I look into the mirror he's holding me against.

His eyes are so dark right now. His blazing gaze is stripping me bare.

The heat from his body against my back is making my pussy clench.

Voices from outside clear some of the thick fog in my head. "Alan…. What if—" I moan when he presses a kiss over my hammering pulse. "—they hear us?"

"Either you give up that dress and we walk out of here now or I could fuck you hard and you can keep this dress. The choice is yours."

I don't even hesitate. "I'm keeping the dress."

His jaw ticks. I know he's pissed but I couldn't be happier. It means this man is my equal and he respects my choices.

With a hand between my shoulder blades, he lowers me. He keeps pushing until my palms are braced against the mirror and my ass is pushed out.

He nuzzles my neck before whispering in my ear, "You were a very bad girl today. What am I going to do with you?"

His hand disappears inside my dress and palms the globe of my ass. I push into his hand, craving more of his touch.

I don't believe that this is my reality. I never thought I'll have a hot, British man fondling me in a fitting room.

I can feel his hardness through our clothes and I try to wiggle my ass against his hardness.

His guttural moan urges me on to grind against him but before I could shimmy my hips, my body is rocked forward and I feel a sting of pain in my ass cheek. Shit. It hurt!

He caresses the skin for a few seconds. I screw my eyes shut when the touch disappears, knowing he is going to spank my still-smarting ass.

The second one hurts more and I whimper.

The sound of his palm cracking against my skin reverberates in the small room. "A-Alan. Someone might hear…" *you spanking me.*

He doesn't talk. After spanking my ass a couple more times, he tears my thong off me.

I cry out when he slams inside me in one violent thrust.

There's no foreplay required as I am dripping from his spankings.

I press my right cheek against the cool mirror as he fucks me into oblivion.

He pulls my left knee up and places it on the round gray dressing room ottoman and bends me some more.

I moan with pain and pleasure as he relentlessly drives into me.

He grips my hair at the nape as he hits all the right spots. I can feel my orgasm building.

It's close. So close that I can almost taste it. My tongue peeks out to wet my lips as I close my eyes in ecstasy.

Alan lets out a curse before coming deep inside me. We decided it was for the better for me to get on the pill so it wasn't the first time he came inside me.

What bothers me is he didn't make me come.

Pulling free, he helps me up and tucks himself in. "Get changed. I'll wait for you outside." He turns to leave.

"Umm, Alan… I didn't…"

"Come. I know. This was your punishment. Remember this day before defying me again."

I'm quiet as I dig into my purse for my keys.

Unlocking the door, I get inside and turn to face him, gripping the doorframe.

"I'll see you tomorrow morning." He bends his head and kisses my forehead.

I try not to feel the stab of disappointment. He doesn't leave until I have closed the door behind me.

I understand why he's so pissed at me. I may have manipulated him into attending Mason's engagement party next week.

Mason is Serah's childhood friend. In no time, he and his boyfriend, Lucas became our best friends. They invited all of us including Alan but as he didn't know them personally, he was hesitant to go.

Knowing how possessive Alan is, I knew he wouldn't like the idea of me going to LA and attending one of Lucas's infamous parties.

Lucas is a fashion designer, meaning he has lots of model friends.

That means there will be many male models and aspiring actors. He wouldn't like me parading the party in that sexy dress so he has to come with us.

At least that's what I was aiming for. Now I feel like a fool. What if he doesn't come?

I am still leaning against the closed door when there's a knock.

I turn and open the door and Alan's piercing gaze greets me.

"A-Alan…" I take a step back when he pushes the door open and stalks into the apartment.

"You little minx." The corner of his lips lifts slightly in an amused smirk.

Did he figure out my game? When he continues to stalk forward, I feel a surge of thrill.

"What are you doing?"

Instead of answering my question like a normal person, he bends and grabs me around my waist. Shouldering my stomach, he lifts me off the floor.

"Alan!" I cry out and watch upside down as he carries me over his shoulder to the bedroom.

"I'll make it up to you for denying you your release but don't think I am unaware of your little games." He spanks me. "You're going to do as I say from now on if you want me on that trip."

Yes! Alan and I would be in LA for the whole weekend. I'll make sure he relaxes on the trip instead of working through the weekends like he usually does.

I bite back a surprised yelp when he tosses me on my bed but can't keep the grin off my face.

"Get naked." He orders before kicking my bedroom door shut.

CHAPTER 24

Rochelle

Turning on my side, I groan when I feel the soreness between my legs.

I blink awake with the feeling of being watched and find Alan in all his naked glory, propped on his elbow watching me.

I bite my lower lip, trying not to gawk at him. "How long have I been out?"

"About an hour."

"You should've woken me up."

"I wore you out. You needed the nap, baby." He tucks a few errant locks behind my ear.

Scooting closer to him, I push him to his back and use his bicep as a pillow.

This is so good. I am loving the way we are cuddling while rain splatters my bedroom window.

But I know he will leave soon. We made huge progress in the acquisition. The owner of the hotel has finally agreed to sell.

I don't know much as I have been tangled in my studies, but I know enough that he is going to sign the rights in the coming days.

I trace circles on his chest, the silver heart charm of my bracelet grazing his skin in the process.

Wait a minute. *Bracelet?*

I sit up and trace the bracelet. It's the one I lost in the café. How?

Alan pushes up and leans against the headboard.

"I thought I lost it," I mumble absentmindedly.

"Seems like you didn't," he murmurs. His gaze rove over me.

"Yeah…" I lock eyes with him. He explains in brief how he found my bracelet tangled in his sweater the day we first met.

It feels like our story has come full circle.

That day, I thought I had lost my chance with him along with my bracelet.

Who'd have thought this simple dainty thing would find its way back to me through the love of my life?

I lean forward, my lips brushing his mouth in a soft kiss. "I love you."

I didn't mean to say it out loud but for how long can I keep my love hidden? It was bound to happen.

I can't take my words back and I don't want to. I know it's too soon.

For him perhaps, but for me, it feels like ages. It feels like I have been in love with him since forever.

He deepens the kiss. His teeth nibble on my lower lip as his hand fists in my hair.

After a few moments, he breaks the kiss and presses his forehead to mine.

"I have to go." His voice is warm and gentle. I give a small nod and pull back to place a chaste kiss on his forehead.

I watch him as he climbs off the bed and bends down to collect his discarded clothes.

When he is fully dressed, he walks back to bed and runs his knuckles down my cheek.

He presses one last kiss on my lips before leaving.

When I hear the closing of the front door, something squeezes in my chest.

I close my eyes with a sad smile when I realize he never said those words back.

It has been three days since I confessed my love to Alan.

He is acting like that confession never happened. There's no change in his behavior which makes it very difficult for me.

While on the outside I am behaving normally, on the inside, I am trying to survive the emotional turbulence.

I didn't reckon not hearing it back from Alan—who means the entire world to me—could be this painful.

It's a little awkward that he now knows about my true feelings and I have no idea about his. I did have a talk with him about being exclusive and he was upfront about being with only me.

But it's still different from love.

Maybe I am just overthinking it.

Shaking off the somberness, I step out of the elevator and walk to my cubicle. I am not even settled down when Olivia approaches me.

"Rochelle, Mr. Will is in a very important meeting—" Wait a second. The meeting was scheduled for tomorrow.

She thrusts something in my hand. "—This is a list. You have an hour to get them, okay?" In a frantic hurry, she moves past me.

Seems like this was an impromptu meeting.

I read the list of refreshments.

Coffee, with and without caffeine

Bottled water

Damn, the list is thorough. She even mentioned the water brands.

I hope I could fetch those things in an hour.

After I returned with the things on the list, I was dreading she would ask me to serve as well. Not that it would be my first time doing that. I have done things like that as it is a part of being an intern, but I was sweaty from running around.

I take a relieved breath when I learn she had hired a few people to cater to the business associates. Olivia is efficient in what she does.

I hope she doesn't find out that I didn't exactly follow her instructions.

I had no time left for getting one item on the list, so I improvised.

I am biting my nails by the time the meeting is wrapped up.

When the conference room door opens, and people start pouring out, I take a breath of relief.

While everyone tries to get a peek at the mysterious person who had Alan all worked up, I lean back in my chair and close my eyes.

They didn't spot the difference in one of the items on the list. *Phew.*

"What a pleasant surprise," My lids snap open at the familiar voice.

"Mr. Taylor?" I jump up from my seat and round the cubicle to reach him.

"Ms. Moore," It feels like a lifetime ago when I used to work at the café. I made few friends there, one of them is Mr. Taylor, er… Michael.

"What are you doing here?" The moment I ask the question is when realization dawns on me.

He's the owner of the hotel Alan was adamant about buying.

"You two know each other?" Alan strides over to where we are standing. His gaze shifts between Michael and me.

"Yes. Michael is a regular at the café where I used to work."

"Small world. By the way, I loved the cookies." He smiles and I dart my eyes at Alan who's watching our interaction with a puzzled look.

I must come clean. "Actually, I was running out of time so instead of buying one of the refreshments on the list, I decided to grab the homemade sugar-free cookies from my place as I was in the area."

I grimace when I spot Olivia giving me the stink eye. That means she heard everything.

From the corner of my eye, I see men in suits approaching Mr. Taylor. They whisper something in his ear.

"I'll take your leave. I have some matters to attend to."

He turns to Alan. "It was a pleasure doing business with you, Mr. Will. I appreciate the revised strategy. You have my gratitude."

"It wouldn't have been possible if it weren't for Ms. Moore's advice. She made me ponder in a way that could benefit us both. This resulted the change in my decision of not buying the hotel and instead becoming a partner. You get to keep your heritage in the family, and I get to implement new policies to expand it."

"You were looking out for your friend even without being aware of it." Mr. Taylor gives me a soft smile.

"I-I... it was nothing. I can't and will not take credit for Alan's hard work. I might have played a small part in this but there's no comparing it with the brilliance of how Alan thought of this alternative and the way he implemented it. I am so proud of him."

I go crimson when I realize I was praising Alan in front of the entire office.

Alan watches me with an expression that makes my heart flutter.

I know that look. I've seen it countless times when he's seconds away from ravaging me.

Clearing my throat, I say, "Congratulations, Michael." Mr. Taylor gives me a knowing smile before nodding at us and leaving.

"In my office, Ms. Moore." Alan strides toward his office.

Once we're inside, he orders, "Lock the door, love."

I was so right. Suppressing a smile, I do just that.

CHAPTER 25

Rochelle

Alan and I are playing a game. Game of sneaking glances at each other.

Asher, Emily, Alan, and I joined Tatum and Serah on their private jet to LA.

The entire flight the couples were getting all lovey-dovey while Alan and I had to maintain our distance.

It wasn't decided, we simply assumed we would keep our relationship on the hush.

So here we are, trying to act nonchalant about each other's presence.

SINFUL LOVE

When we landed in Los Angeles, it was easy to forget about our predicament for a little while.

Lucas and Mason's happiness was contagious.

Mason and Serah are childhood friends. He had to go through a lot of hardships to finally get to his happiness.

Not only he is a well-known photographer, but he's now also marrying Lucas; the love of his life.

Their cute two-story house is in a gated community.

Upon entering, I was in awe of the arrangements. They went all out.

After the brunch with the happy couple and their family, we enjoyed the small get-together in their backyard.

When the guests left, the young crowd decided to move the party to one of the exclusive clubs in Los Angeles.

I was reluctant because of my age, but Lucas said the club belongs to a friend and as I was a non-drinker it was okay to go with them.

I changed into the dress Alan bought. It was perfect for the nightclub and... let's just say Alan was *not* happy about it by the way he was grunting instead of talking. Glaring at anyone who dared to stare at me for more than two seconds.

Asher assumed he was jet-lagged and suggested he stay at the hotel. But Alan insisted on coming with us, saying he was in the mood to party.

Asher was left baffled because Alan's words contradicted his glaring eyes. The scene almost had me giggling.

Which brings us to the present. I stay close to Emily as we are escorted by one of the men—who seem to be a bouncer—inside the club.

We didn't have to wait in line as Lucas directly strolled to the front and talked to the gate person.

I can feel Alan's presence behind me, and it gives me a sense of security. Since yesterday, he has always stayed within a close distance of me.

It isn't enough as I am being deprived by his affection, his touch but his nearness still warms my heart.

He is even more tempting now in denim jeans and a black button-down shirt.

My urges are put to test tonight. It's taking a lot of effort to force my steps forward instead of turning around.

"This is so exciting!" Emily grins at me.

The massive multidimensional oval lighting structure overhead is changing colors by the beats of the music blaring through the club.

I am kind of shocked to find the place packed with people at eleven p.m. but then, I have never gone clubbing before so I can't really tell whether this is normal or not.

"I agree!" says Serah and I hear Tatum grumbling something. He is being overprotective. Serah's words.

Tatum's protectiveness has reached an all-time high since she got pregnant.

The man leads us to the U-shaped booth which gives us an unobstructed view of the dance floor.

Apart from us eight, there are five of the happy couple's friends—three men and two women— with us. And as I don't know them, I sit beside Emily.

Alan pushes one of the men not so subtly to the side when he tries to sit next to me and takes a seat beside me. My breath hitches when his thigh brushes against mine.

I crane my neck to the left when Serah starts to tell a story from her and Mason's childhood days.

I suddenly feel a tug on my hair tie before it's pulled free from my ponytail, my long hair falling all around me.

I feel the brush of Alan's lips on my bare shoulder. "That's better." His hand snakes around and grips my waist.

Thank God, the lighting is muted, the dim purple light overhead is not bright enough for everyone to notice that I am practically on his lap.

"W-what are you doing—"

"Shh. We can't let anyone see that seductive neck of yours." The timbre of his voice makes me shiver.

"Alan…"

"I miss you, love." He buries his face in my hair and inhales deeply.

I turn then. "I miss you too," I whisper before licking my lips quickly. His eyes drop to mouth.

His breathing turns ragged and even in the darkened club, I can see how his pupils dilate. Like he's already picturing how he wants to devour my lips.

Why does the thought of kissing him in front of everyone is not scaring me away? My eyes flutter close and I draw closer to him, silently begging him to kiss me.

"Ohmygod! *RJ* is here!" I hear one of Lucas's girlfriends exclaim.

I jerk away from Alan and clear my throat.

"Raleigh!" One of the leggy brunette gasps.

I lift my eyes to look at the person who had beautiful girls like them gasping for breath.

He's tall and lean with broad shoulders. With dark brown hair and sun-kissed skin, he looks like one of the models I saw during the backyard get-together earlier.

He is wearing a stylish leather jacket over a slim-fit white t-shirt and dark wash jeans.

"You finally got the time to make it, asshole?" Mason smirks before pushing to his feet to give Raleigh a hug.

"I'm here for Lucas." He winks at Lucas who squeals before jumping up to squeeze him in a hug.

"Remember I told you about my friends from New York? Guys, this is Raleigh Jackson, my dearest friend. He works at one of the hottest Ad agencies in the city, Kim Advertising. Raleigh, meet Asher Will…" Lucas starts introducing us all.

He greets everyone with a warm smile, a cute dimple teasing his cheek.

I am still stuck over the fact that he is not a GQ magazine model and instead works behind the scenes.

"… That's our cutie Rochelle, Emily's sister."

"Hello, Rochelle." The way he emphasizes my name while smirking is kind of flirtatious.

His baby blue eyes twinkle when Alan stiffens beside me.

"Hi." I smile.

"RJ, Come sit with us!" the girls wave him over and he grins, showcasing his pearly white teeth. This guy knows the effect he has on the female population, and he loves it.

"There's no room for me." He pushes his lower lip out, pouting mockingly.

"I can sit on your lap." I turn to watch the brunette, my eyes bulging out of their sockets. She rubs her lips together before giving Raleigh a sensuous smile.

My gaze bounces back at Raleigh when he chuckles. His eyes fall on Alan before sliding to me, a mischievous gleam shining in them.

He strides in my direction and sits down on the booth table right in front of me. "This is better, no?"

The girl whines but he pays them no attention.

Alan

I fist my hands to control myself from punching his square jaw.

The wanker has captured the ladies' attention by his smooth-talking and tales of his adventures.

I try to ignore it when Rochelle inhales a breath in awe. He is not even trying and yet he has everyone's focus.

Maybe it's his personality that draws people in.

Not once did I find his gaze roaming over Rochelle's revealing dress. Maybe I am being irrational.

My stare flickers over the irritated look on Asher and Tatum's faces. It's like looking into the mirror.

Maybe they are feeling threatened by Raleigh like I am.

Yes, threatened. I am man enough to accept it.

When the ladies laugh again at a joke he cracked, I am done with this bullshit.

"Rochelle, your favourite song is playing."

Her brow creases. "It is?"

I nod. "Why don't you girls join Rochelle on the dance floor?"

Asher gives me a subtle nod like he gets what I am trying to do before jumping in. "That's a great idea, brother."

"B-but I don't want to——"

"How do you know about her favourite song anyway?" Emily raises her brows.

"She was humming a similar tune in the office a few days ago."

"Okay! I am always up for dancingggg!" Emily stands.

I give Rochelle a push. "Off you go."

"Don't tire yourself much." Tatum kisses Serah's forehead.

Raleigh watches everything with amused eyes. "Why's the couple still here? Don't tell me you are going to avoid the dance floor like usual." He smirks at Mason.

"Like hell you will." Lucas glares at Mason before tugging him toward the dance floor.

Why did he provoke Lucas like that? Why is he trying to make them scarce?

I am good at reading people but for some reason, I can't read him.

When everyone's on the dance floor, Tatum and Asher scoot over to where I am sitting.

We don't even need to communicate, it's crystal clear that we want to crack this charming persona of his.

All three of us study him intently.

The purpose is to make him sweat but instead, he gets comfortable by leaning one palm on the table he is perched on and lifting the tumbler to his lips with the other hand.

With the infuriating smirk still intact, he regards us over the rim of his glass.

We continue staring at each other for a few minutes. I now know this bastard is not one of those weaklings who crack under pressure.

Giving in, I start. "What do you do again?"

He takes his time swallowing the liquid.

After resting the glass beside his hip, he tilts his head. "I work for Kim Advertising."

"Hmm. I am thinking of investing in the industry. Think I should buy the company you work for?" Tatum challenges.

This feels like a dick measuring contest. Are we that far gone for our women that we are cornering a man now?

If Tatum was aiming for planting a seed of fear in Raleigh, he didn't bite.

His smirk broadens. "Threatening my job, Blackstone?"

"Do I have to?" Tatum asks.

"You can do whatever the hell you want, buddy. It's a free country after all." He shrugs. But then there's a shift in his expression and he leans forward.

"I'll let you in on a secret." He whispers, his eyes mocking. "I wasn't born with a silver spoon in my mouth. I achieved my status in society and position in Kim Advertising by working my ass off. I am not the man you can scare away by these threats. You know why?" He grins before lifting his glass. "Because I am *RJ*. Guess what R stands for."

Asher snorts. "Raleigh."

"Tsk, tsk." Raleigh stops smiling. "It stands for *Ruthless*."

The silence stretches.

Raleigh's expression goes from serious to sunshine in the blink of an eye. "I know where you guys are coming from but I can't help the attention I get." He shrugs a shoulder. "I am harmless. Scout's honour!" He raises his hands in mock surrender.

"I need another drink. You guys want me to get you something?" he gives us a friendly smile which kind of makes me feel like shit.

At our silence, he stands and leaves, still smiling.

"Damn," Asher says.

"I know." Tatum nods. "I get crazy jealous when someone even breathes near my wife. I went too far." He shakes his head.

Raleigh earned my respect. He not only survived under the pressure of the three most powerful men in this club, but he also managed to render us speechless.

That doesn't mean my little doll will escape her punishment.

She gave him a smile that belonged to me. She will pay for this.

I get the chance when Rochelle starts walking towards the farther side of the club. Excusing myself, I follow her.

CHAPTER 26

Rochelle

We cheer as Mason twirls Lucas. They look so happy.

I smile when Emily hooks her arms around their necks, belting out the lyrics of the song. Mason chuckles when Lucas joins, singing his heart out.

I move to the beats uncomfortably. The dress sliding up with every move of my body is pissing me off. I reach down and subtly tug it down again.

It was odd of Alan to rush me to the dance floor out of the blue.

I glance at our booth and watch Tatum, Asher, and Alan glaring at Raleigh.

I stop moving and crane my neck to inspect the scene before me.

I can't see Raleigh's face as he's still perched on the table with his back to the dance floor.

Lucas tugs my arm. "Ro, show me your moves."

Distracted, I try to mimic his steps, laughing when he starts twerking.

I immerse myself in dancing. Surrounded by my friends, I laugh and find myself having a good time.

I dance away, moving my hips, encouraged by my girls. Emily is drunk judging by her flushed cheeks and stumbled steps. She had too many cocktails during the course of the night.

"I need a group selfie," Emily shouts.

"I second that." Lucas throws his hands up.

"Let's head to the booth. You won't get any good pictures with all the movements around us," Mason is referring to the pushes of the dancing bodies around us. He has a fair point.

"Is that a challenge, Mase?" she smirks before pulling out her phone from her clutch. Aiming it up with her outstretched hand, she starts snapping selfies, instructing us to pout.

Mason just shakes his head at her fondly before posing for her pictures.

When the DJ changes the song to another fast number, I stop dancing. My heels are killing me.

Desperately wanting a breather, I shout over the music to inform them that I am stepping off the dance floor.

I head to the back of the club through the throng of people, pushing through them to search the way to the bathroom.

I am walking down the hallway, still looking for the restroom when someone grabs my arm.

Alan.

He starts dragging me behind him and pushes a door open before pulling me inside.

He locks the door to what I now know is a bathroom.

"What's wrong?" My breathing hitches when he lifts his stormy eyes to watch me. He uncuffs his shirt sleeves and starts rolling them up.

I sink my teeth on my lower lip when I get a full view of his veiny arms.

I take a step back when he takes purposeful steps toward me. I start backing up until my ass hits the vanity.

My neck cranes when I tilt my head to maintain eye contact, his height and broad shoulders shadowing me.

Alan is not touching me. There's still an inch of space that is preventing my chest from grazing his and yet I am growing damp between my legs. He doesn't even have to touch me to make me wet.

His eyes darken. "Did you enjoy flirting with him?"

I frown at his ridiculous question. What is he talking about? Is it about Raleigh?

"You smiled at him, love."

"I was just being polite, Alan." I roll my eyes. He is acting like a caveman right now. "We should head back. They will start looking for us." I manage to squeeze past him and head for the door, but he grabs me and swings me around to face him.

He then slips his hand around my waist and pulls me to his body.

My nipples harden. The thin dress wasn't made for a bra, so I decided not to wear one.

Tipping my chin up by his fingers, he leans down. "I think I wasn't finished talking." He says in that authoritative tone. My stomach flips, heart palpitating.

"A-Alan."

"Were you trying to make me jealous, baby?" He breathes against my lips.

"No," I gasp when I feel his free hand reaching between my thighs. My eyes fall shut when his fingers brush against my thong. The familiar wave of heat surges up my body.

"Who owns this pussy?"

I shake my head. Why does he have such a dirty mouth?

His hands abandon me. My eyes fly open when he picks me up and sits me on the edge of the vanity counter. My weak protests turn into moans the second he presses his lips on my neck.

I moan loudly when he licks and sucks on my pulse. I reach for him, my nails clawing at his shoulders.

My knees spread on their own accord, making room for him.

He gets this hint as he steps closer but tears his mouth away from my neck to stare at me, my half-mast eyes locking on his lust-filled ones.

I wet my lips, waiting with bated breath for his next move. "You're right. We must return." He takes a step back.

What is he doing? Isn't he going to… finish what he started? Is this my punishment for not answering his question?

I don't give him a chance to move. Fisting his shirt, I yank him toward me and wrap my legs around his narrow waist. I tip my head, trying to reach his tempting lips. "You."

Not bothering to bend down to kiss me, Alan cocks an eyebrow. I grit my teeth.

"Alan, please." I try to tug him down, but he doesn't budge.

He is clever, I'll give him that. I have used the 'please' strategy so many times that he is now immune to it.

I can feel the warmth flooding my cheeks as I prepare myself to say it. "You own my pussy." As soon I say it, I bury my bright red face in his chest.

I bite him over his shirt when I hear him chuckle. I wince. Is he made up of steel?

His fingers fist in my hair and tugs until I am looking at him. "Don't do that unless you want to get my marks all over your porcelain skin."

Why does the thought of him giving me hickeys is filling me with thrill?

He might've seen my thoughts about his threat written all over my face because his eyes get darker.

Palming my ass, he pulls me forward and slams his mouth down on mine, his erection rubbing against my soaked thong evokes the hunger in me that only he could sate.

He bites down on my lower lip hard before pulling away. Anger igniting in his gaze, "You're mine. Understand?"

I cup his jaw. "Yes, only yours. Always." I love you, I try to tell him with my eyes.

He responds by claiming my mouth. I thread my fingers in his hair as our tongues taste each other after two days of depravity.

In this bathroom, he is mine. Away from everyone's watchful eyes, I can have him.

I am in heaven because I am in his arms. I take my fill. Inhaling him, tasting him until there is only him ruling all my senses.

I almost cry in relief when his hand trails underneath my dress again. This time he doesn't tease me. Still kissing me, he rips my panties off me with a violent yank.

One of his hands finds my strap and works it down while the other plays with my pussy.

Breaking the kiss, he trails his lips down my throat, then to my collarbone. Sucking the skin in his mouth, he moves down to my now exposed breast. He sucks gently on the nipple.

Just when I thought he was going to be rough, he changes his plans. His movement on my pussy slows.

He drives me mad by sucking each nipple slowly like he is worshipping them.

My hips grind against his hand as I throw my head back on a tortured cry.

He unglues his mouth from my now sensitive breasts. "Frustrating, isn't it? That's how my last two days have been. And then to top it all of, you smiled at someone who isn't me."

"Alan, for god's sake," I whimper. "Please, don't torment me anymore."

"What do you want?"

"You," I sob.

"You're mine."

"I am. I love you, Alan." He stills against me but then with a roar, he unbuckles his pants and buries himself in me to the hilt in one go.

I cry out as he fucks me hard. He pinches my nipple as he pumps into me deeper. My mouth hangs open in a silent cry as my body rocks back and forth on the marble.

One of my heels falls on the bathroom floor from the force Alan is thrusting inside of me.

"Aah," I moan as he hits the sweet spot that makes my toes curl.

Leaning forward, I wrap my hands around his neck and bury my nose under the curve of his jaw, licking his Adam's apple.

He groans and his strokes become frantic. My feet dig into his back as I move my hips, fucking him back.

Sweat coats my forehead but we don't stop. My breathing quickens as I feel my orgasm building.

Alan senses it and pulls back to watch as my body twitches from pleasure as I come.

I jerk in his embrace as the aftershocks rip through me. He soaks it all up like always.

He loves watching me submit to the pleasure. My orgasm triggers his as he curses and lets out a guttural moan. The sound is so erotic, it sends me into another climax.

He holds onto me until I stop trembling, his own body shakes as we both slowly come down from the high.

I wince when he pulls out of me. He then helps me clean up.

Minutes later when we are done straightening out our clothes, he pulls me in his arms.

I close my eyes, trying not to think about how he still didn't say those words back.

A knock at the door draws my attention from my thoughts.

We go completely still when the knock comes again before I hear the familiar voice. "Anybody in there?"

Emily.

I pull away to look at him with wide eyes. Panic rises in me when she calls out again. "Is anybody in there? I asked you something! Hellooooo?"

"Fuck! What do I do?" I whisper-shout.

He raises his eyebrow.

"I swear sometimes. I can't handle being under pressure."

He puts a finger on his lips, gesturing me to be silent, and moves to the door to put his ear against it.

After a minute he straightens. When he goes to open the door, I grab his wrist.

"She is gone. I heard the retreating footsteps. We should get out now."

He opens the door at my nod and we leave the bathroom and walk the way we came from.

Emily meets us on the way with Asher and a bouncer in tow.

"I'm telling you it's locked from the inside!" Emily slurs.

She rushes to my side when she spots me. "Rooooo!"

She stumbles into me and I almost lose my balance. Alan's hand darts out and steadies me. I look up to thank him but he is already stepping away. His face is strangely blank. No trace of my lover can be found in him.

The façade of indifference is so perfect, I begin doubting the events in the bathroom as a figment of my imagination.

Emily presses a sloppy kiss on my cheek. "I missed you, Ro. Where were you? I was looking for you."

I smile at her. "I am right here. Let's go." She nods but then shakes her head.

"I need to pee but the bathroom is locked!" She glares at the bouncer like it's his fault.

"I'll check. Just a moment." The bouncer approaches the bathroom and we all follow. He turns the knob and the door opens.

"How did you do that?! It was locked." Her eyes are wide as saucers. Asher bites his lip to suppress his laugh.

"You're right, baby but now that it's unlocked, why don't you go inside and I'll wait here."

"Fine."

Asher turns to us after she steps inside. He looks at me then at Alan.

"What were you two doing together?"

My pulse races as I smell suspicion in his question.

"I was out for a quick smoke." His tone lacks concern. It doesn't escape me how he skillfully omitted me from his response when the question was about us.

"I just needed a breather so I was exploring the club and ran into Alan."

If he suspects my lie, he doesn't talk about it. Emily exits the bathroom after few minutes, glaring at the door in the process.

"I swear it was locked." She mumbles. Asher tucks her under his arm and kisses her forehead. Murmuring things to her that make her giggle.

I watch them with a smile then peer at Alan and find him looking at them.

As if sensing the weight of my gaze, he locks eyes with me. Can he read the longing etched on my face?

Watching my sister being adored and loved by Asher makes my heart greedy. It wants to feel it too. It wants more than sex. I want to hold his hand in public too.

In this moment, I realize that keeping our relationship secret is not the thing I want anymore.

His gaze lingers on me for a beat or two before he snatches it away.

Pulling out his phone, he saunters off. They both follow him out.

With a resigned sigh, I trail behind them.

CHAPTER 27

A week later

Rochelle

I pad over to the walk-in closet in Alan's bedroom. "Can I tell them over the phone?" I wring my hands.

Alan pulls the tie drawer and looks at me.

"The black one." I motion to the silk tie.

Grabbing it, he approaches me and hands it to me. It's a routine we've adopted. He loves it when I do it for him.

Placing the tie around his neck, I cross the wide end over the thinner one. "I don't have to see them in person for this." I peer up at him before adding, "Right?"

My internship ended with Will's Valley as the acquisition was now complete.

Knowing how much I am into cooking, he now wants me to talk to my parents about dropping out of school to opt for professional culinary training.

I reasoned with him that it would be a rash decision. I don't want to disappoint my family.

But like he pointed out, I would never know until I talk to them.

Yesterday was the last day of my internship. From today onwards Alan would operate from Hotel Paradise.

The name is soon going to change to Paradise Valley. This was Alan's idea and it would be the first time he would compromise with Will's Valley's brand name.

He came up with this idea when he was thinking from Mr. Taylor's perspective.

The hotel was in Michael's family for more than a hundred years. It held sentimental values and that's the reason he was hesitant to sell.

Through Alan's renewed contract, everyone benefits from this acquisition now.

So now he is getting ready to head to the hotel. He practically ordered me to visit my parents today.

He knows about my dream of becoming a well-known chef someday and he wants to see it happening. He wants me to live my dream one day because he believes in me.

But how am I going to bring this up? How am I going to convince them?

Sliding the knot upwards, I flip his collar down. "Are you going to answer—" His lips shut me up. His tongue slips between my lips as he deepens the kiss.

Before I could kiss him back, he breaks it and leans back.

"You and I both know you are going to do this. You're the bravest, and the strongest girl I know, Rochelle. It was your fearlessness that brought us together.

"I would have wasted god knows how long thinking about others' opinions and 'what ifs' but you took the chance. On us. Now, I want you to take a chance on your dreams."

Eyes welling up with emotions, I crush my face into his chest.

His arms come around me and he hugs me tighter. I can spend an eternity in the cocoon of his strong and warm arms.

"I might spend the night at my parents'," I warn him after pulling away.

He smiles at that. "It's a price I can pay."

John drives me to Brooklyn.

SINFUL LOVE

I squirm in the plush backseat, my ass sore from the spanking I received when I argued about taking the subway. It wasn't even an argument because it requires two people. Alan doesn't argue his points, he acts upon them.

The corner of my lips tips up. Every day he does something that makes me fall in love with him all over again.

He thinks I am the bravest girl. He doesn't know that he is the one who introduced me to this new side of me.

I had no idea I could be someone who could love so freely. A girl who can express her feelings to the man of her dreams without thinking of the repercussion.

Before, I used to think I won't be like the sappy girl who dreams of a white picket fence and having 2.5 kids.

I thought I was a practical girl who wouldn't break apart at the thought of separating from Alan. I guess I was deluding myself.

I can't imagine leaving him. I can't.

While it still hurts that he isn't in love with me yet, I take solace in his tender care.

I will take everything he can give me, hoping one day he will give me his heart too.

"We're here, ma'am." John gets out and comes around to open my door.

279

Climbing off the car, I swing my purse on my shoulder.

"Thank you for the ride. And please call me Rochelle." He gives me a nod, his eyes kind.

When he doesn't move, I frown.

"I can't leave until you're inside the house, ma'am... Rochelle. Mr. Will's orders."

My mouth falls open. Alan's protectiveness is a bit too much sometimes.

True to his words, John stays until Mom opens the door.

She holds her arms out to me. "Ro, honey." Her hazel eyes light up.

Dropping the bag at the threshold, I eagerly step forward to hug her.

"Hi, Mom,"

"Emily is already here." She tells me as we cross the living room.

I knew she would be here because I had called her as well. I wanted everyone here.

I hear her voice coming from the hallway. "She is in the kitchen?" I raise my brow and Mom starts laughing.

"Don't worry. Your dad is with her." I still remember the day when she tried cooking for the first time and almost lit the house on fire.

"I made your favorite soup—"

"Mom... I need to talk to you guys." It is better if I get straight to the point. I don't know if I could sit through lunch without being sick from nervousness.

"Oh. Sure, honey. I'll call them." It's a code word for 'I am going to discuss this with dad and Emily in the kitchen'.

She is worried. It is so unlike me to summon all my family members to talk. They had to take a day off for me.

She disappears into the hallway and I use that moment to take in the house I have technically spent my whole life in.

For outsiders, it may be an ordinary-looking house with classic-colored walls, wooden floors, and old-fashioned furniture.

But for me, it is a symbol of warmth and love.

I recall the time I used to stand by the wall of the living room with my crayons and draw stick figures of my family.

It's not been too long since I moved out but it feels like it.

I wait, sitting on the couch, the fear evaporating from my body.

Maybe my childhood house is providing me the courage. Or maybe it's the sight of them coming out.

Emily flops beside me. She pinches my cheek gently in greeting but other than that she stays silent.

Emily and silence can never be in the same room. That only means she sensed something.

"My favorite daughter," Dad grins as he bends down to give me a quick hug.

After everyone's settled, I fill my lungs with a long breath. "I have decided I am going to drop out of school." I blurt in one breath.

Silence.

My gaze drops to my interlinked fingers in my lap.

I did it. I told them.

"What?!" Mom shrills.

"Let her speak, Mom."

A hand enters my vision and settles on my joined hands. "Go on, kiddo," Emily murmurs.

"I want to become a chef."

"Why didn't you tell me before?" Emily asks gently.

"You're my role model, Em. I wanted to be like you. Confident and career-driven but I couldn't turn my back on the one thing that has always had my heart. Cooking." I lift my gaze at my stunned parents.

"Can you guys support me in my decision? I didn't want to disappoint you all but—"

"Oh, you silly, silly girl." Mom rushes to me and takes a seat to my right.

Cupping my face, she brushes a loose tendril away. "You can never disappoint us, Rochelle. Why didn't you tell us, honey? Do what makes your heart smile. If cooking does that for you then who are we to object?"

"Your mother is right. I always want to see both of my daughters happy."

"Oh, Dad." I push to my feet and run to squeeze him in a hug. "Don't tell your mother, but you're a better cook than her." He winks at me.

"I heard that." She grumbles.

"Can we please eat now? I am starving!" Shouts Emily and we all break into laughter.

Can someone pinch me? It is hard to believe that I not only told them about quitting school, but I also got their support.

I was planning to stay here for the night but now there is a change of plan.

I want to share this good news with Alan. I would not be able to sleep if I don't tell him in person.

He was right. All I had to do was take a chance. Now, I won't have to live with regrets.

I hang out with them for a few more hours before leaving. He must be home by now.

I don't remember the journey to his building. I am feeling gleeful and so happy that I could twirl in the lobby right now.

Quickly punching in the code to his penthouse, I look up at the illuminating numbers. Willing the elevator to take me to him fast.

My toes wiggles in my sneakers with anticipation. No heels or pencil skirts today. I am wearing a simple green buttoned placket t-shirt with black jeans.

The elevator door opens and I step inside the penthouse.

Walking through the quiet foyer, I enter the massive living room area.

A large grin almost splits my face in two when I spot him.

He is facing away from me. I tip-toe toward him and when I am a few feet away, he pivots on his heels abruptly.

My shoulders slump and I push out my lower lip. One of the disadvantages of having a partner with sharp instincts is that you can never prank him. "Alan—"

"Ms. Moore, what are you doing here?"

He places his hands in his pockets. I draw in a quick breath as I take in his changed demeanor.

Oh. Is he trying to prank *me?* His great acting skills sometimes put me in a doubt.

I narrow my eyes at him, trying my best to appear angry but I am in such a good mood it's difficult to even act to be mad.

I just want to hug him right now and kiss him until we both are breathless. After that, I will share my good news.

His hand darts out to stop me when I start toward him again. My smile falters. "Alan?"

I notice his posture and stare at his blank expression. "How did you get in?"

His coldness shakes me. My fingers wrap around the silver bracelet, trying to draw in some strength.

"Who is this girl?" the disdain-filled, unfamiliar voice chills me further.

A woman who appears to be in her early sixties steps forward from behind Alan. Her grey hair is styled into a bob and her petite figure is covered in an expensive dress.

I feel inferior as I am the only one dressed in cheap clothes but what kills me is her scornful gaze.

Her dark brown eyes match Alan's and it doesn't take long for me to figure out who she is.

Alan's mother.

"Her name's Rochelle Moore. I was mentoring her as a favour for Asher's girlfriend." His detached tone makes me stumble a little.

"Do all your employees have a free pass to stroll inside your house whenever they please?" Her gaze flicks over my clothes, her lips pull down in distaste when she takes in my sneakers.

Alan ignores his mother and speaks again. "Let's talk in my study."

"There's no need. This was a mistake. I'm so sorry for the disturbance, sir." I smile at his mother. "I apologize, ma'am." She huffs and rolls her eyes.

My eyes flit to Alan's face. His nostrils flares slightly but other than that he doesn't say anything.

I take a shaky step back, nodding again, I turn to leave.

CHAPTER 28

Rochelle

The person we love the most in this world has the ultimate power to hurt you the most. It feels like my heart has been sliced open and I feel helpless because even bloodied, it is still beating for him.

The first tear slips down my cheek the moment the elevator door cages me in, leaving me in the much-needed solitude. I take a deep breath to steady myself.

The mirrored walls of the elevator taunt me by showing me my reality through my reflection from all four sides. Pure misery is staring back at me wherever I look and it makes me want to hide.

But would hiding cure the ache which is slowly spreading through my entire body?

I blow a stuttered breath out of my lips and swallow. There has to be a reason behind his actions. I don't want to believe otherwise.

Suppose there was indeed a reason, how could I forget what he said.

Favor. He did a favor for my sister.

In a span of a few minutes, Alan made me feel so insignificant. I bite my lower lip hard when it trembles and the metallic taste of blood floods my mouth.

Right now, I want to be in my sister's arms and cry my eyes out. But doing so would raise suspicions.

What will I tell her? How would I explain that I was sleeping with Alan? The man who is ashamed of me.

I wrap my arms around my middle. I feel so alone.

The elevators door opens on one of the floors and an old lady steps in.

I quickly wipe the tears with my knuckles and try to present her a smile when she greets me with one.

"Bad day?" The plump woman asks with a hint of understanding in her soft eyes.

"Something like that." I choke out and clear my throat to cover it.

I have no grudges against his mother because she was unaware of my identity. But Alan? I don't have any excuses left to defend him.

Part of me wants to run up there and demand the truth. But the bigger part is afraid to hear what he has to say.

Does it make me weak if I say I fear losing him even after what went down?

"Take my advice, never keep expectations from anyone, not even your loved ones. Because we are often let down by them than any outsiders. I am speaking from experience."

Is that it? Am I disappointed in him because I had high expectations?

"But," she continues. "I have also had regrets by jumping to conclusions. If you have even the slightest of possibility to be together then fight for it. Sit and talk it out."

"You don't even know if it's about a person. I can have a bad day about any random thing." I frown, genuinely puzzled by her spot-on guess.

She just smiles. "Those bloodshot eyes are telling quite a different tale."

Silence looms and when the elevator door opens to the lobby, I wait for her to exit first.

"I did say fight for it but don't lose yourself completely in a battle where you're the sole warrior."

Her words keep playing in my mind on an endless loop as I walk through the throng of people.

I halt and take a deep breath, hopelessly trying not to lose it.

Someone crashes into me from behind and I stumble and go down.

There's no one to break my fall this time.

My savior truly abandoned me.

With watery eyes, I stare at my bloodied palms and wince when I stand.

When someone asks if I'm okay, I jerk a nod, swipe at my tears with my forearm, and start walking briskly so I won't burst into sobs.

Alan didn't call.

Many times, I was tempted to pick up my phone to call him but I stopped myself from doing so. I don't want to be the sole warrior fighting for salvaging us.

Us. I don't even know what we are. I am in a nameless relationship.

After last evening's event, I wanted to give up on us but then his voice echoed in my ears.

It was your fearlessness that brought us together.

That night sleep didn't come, so I spent my time reading instead.

I was grateful when Emily called me this afternoon. She wanted to see me. I would have made an excuse if it weren't for the urgency in her voice because I was not in the state to leave the apartment.

I am fidgety as I enter the elevator. The same elevator that saw my happiness and witnessed my heartbreak.

Is he at his penthouse right now? I wonder. Do I text him?

It sucks to have no one to share this with.

The secrecy of our relationship was bothering me before but now, it is evoking something nasty in me.

My mind fills with a thought so disturbing, I smother it before it can grow.

I lift my lips into a smile when the doors start to open, knowing full well Emily is probably waiting on the other side of the doors.

As expected, Emily's blonde hair bounces as she practically runs to me. After giving me the tightest hug, she tugs me through the foyer and to her bedroom.

"Emily! Slow down." I try not to wince and keep up with her pace as she navigates through the stairs and leads me to the master bedroom.

My knee is tormenting me because of the fall. Last night's crying has truly sucked all the stamina in me. I feel drained.

"I need your help." She turns to me once we are inside.

The room is exactly like Alan's except for the color schemes. Where Alan's master was a blend of gold and ivory, this room is colorless. As in it's all black and white. Just like the whole penthouse.

The only thing that stands out is the metal garment rack which is filled with colorful dresses.

"My help?"

"Yes!" she grabs me and manhandles me to sit at the edge of the bed. Then she drags the wheeled garment rack and parks it right in front of me.

"Pick one."

"You do realize you are the fashionista between the two of us, right?" I stare at her with bewilderment.

"Just pick one, will you? I am already under a lot of stress." I take a good look at her and notice the creases in her knee-length casual midi. Her hair is in disarray.

I stand and take her by the shoulders. "Deep breaths, Emily." She narrows her eyes but follows my instruction. "Good. Inhale. Exhale. Yes, do it again."

Once she is calm, I make her sit with me. "Now tell me, what's all this about?"

"Asher and I need to go to dinner tonight."

"Oh, is it with his friends? Or business associates? But you guys work together which means you are familiar with almost all of them. So why are you fretting over it?"

She moves to stand again like she can't tolerate being in one place. She starts pacing. "Lydia is here," she whispers.

I frown. "Who's Lydia?"

She slaps her forehead. "I forgot to tell you. Asher's Mom is in the city."

Oh. I already know that.

"You both are having dinner with her." It's not a question.

"More like I convinced Asher into going. If it wasn't for Alan, he wouldn't—"

"Alan?"

"Yeah. It's his birthday today. He arranged tonight's dinner. Asher strongly refused at first but he caved when I expressed my desire of meeting her."

His birthday.

I let the information prick my still battered heart. I am not upset that he didn't invite me.

I am sad because he snatched away the right to even wish him on his day.

I release a pained breath and blink the tears away.

Incoming footsteps make us both turn toward the door. Asher walks inside, his signature mischievous grin missing in action.

"Hey, Rochelle." He nods at me after dropping a kiss on Emily's temple.

"You have to get ready, Asher! Use the guest bedroom so I don't have to kill you. Because I might."

"What?" he glares at her.

"You're aimlessly strolling through the entire house and I am hyperventilating right now. Trust me you do *not* want to get in my way."

"It would be better than meeting my dearest Mum."

"Don't try to scare me!" she stomps to the ensuite and locks herself in.

Others might have rushed to try to placate her but we both don't even bat an eyelash. Emily is being... Emily.

"Why don't you want to meet your mom?"

"It's not me I'm worried about. If it were up to me, I wouldn't allow Lydia near my Emily."

"But why?"

"Let's just say she can be quite rude. Alan and I are used to her but she can be... harsh sometimes. I can't see Emily's feelings getting hurt." The worry in his eyes is palpable.

He can't see my sister's feelings getting hurt.

But Alan not only saw me getting insulted, but he was also an equal participant.

There's still hope that he did that for a reason. But I won't know what that is until I talk to him in person.

He sighs, his grin returning. "I'll get out of your hair now. I don't want to get killed so young." He shouts the last bit so Emily could hear and grins at me before walking out.

A minute later she comes out of the bathroom. "Is he gone?"

"Yes." I shake my head at her.

"Good, now let's get to work!" She tries few of the pieces before plopping on the bed headfirst.

"Ugh!!! I wish you could come with us!"

"It's a family dinner, Em." I smile wryly.

She groans but sits up when I suggest she try a pale pink dress.

Alan

I force myself to relax. I glance at my watch and frown.

Only ten minutes into this disaster of a birthday dinner and I am ready to get the hell out of here.

My eyes move from the watch to the people I am sharing the table with.

Emily's green eyes meet mine and I feel the dull ache in my chest.

Her gaze triggers the memory of the girl with haunting forest green eyes from yesterday. It's clawing at me and leaving me raw with guilt.

Shame and self-loathing fill me all over again.

Unable to take another bite, I place the fork down. What am I doing here? I was never a fan of celebrating birthdays.

It is not something for a man like me who prefers work over mingling and dinners like these.

Truth be told, I was looking forward to spending this day with Rochelle, but now I don't even know if I have the right to call her.

SINFUL LOVE

Two days ago, when I saw Lydia Will waiting for me in the lobby of my residential building, I couldn't comprehend what to do.

She claimed she flew all the way here for my birthday but I knew better.

Her pretence at displaying motherly love ended the moment she entered my penthouse.

Lydia was furious with how 'poorly' I carried out the acquisition.

She wanted to know why I made such 'drastic' changes.

When I kept regarding her with an impassive expression, she started admonishing me about the loss 'our' goodwill may face.

When she was finished with the ranting, I merely pointed out that I was the owner of the Will empire. It was implied that her opinions weren't needed, I didn't need to voice it and insult her openly.

She was bristling. This was the first time I objected to her interference and knowing me, she was aware I wouldn't repeat myself and take actions that would cost Lydia her lavish lifestyle.

That was the exact moment when I heard the lift doors opening.

I momentarily closed my eyes, wishing it wasn't her. I didn't have to turn to know it was Rochelle.

Lydia's expression displayed her piqued interest in the girl who was slowly becoming the reason of my existence.

Keeping my face drained of any emotion, I turned to face her and broke her heart. It was necessary. She didn't need Lydia to complicate her life.

She possesses power and contacts that could ruin lives with a flick of her wrist. I couldn't let Rochelle be the target.

Rochelle is my weakness and I refused to let Lydia exploit it. I had to do something that wouldn't force my hand into destroying my relationship with Lydia.

So, I did what I thought was right at that time.

To save my relationship with my mother, keep Rochelle out of problems, and my word to Mr. Taylor, I broke her heart.

It's only a matter of few weeks. The renovation work would start soon and Lydia will return to London.

I'll have to maintain some distance from Rochelle.

"You work for my son, am I right?" Lydia asks Emily after taking a sip of her wine.

"Yes, I am his PA."

"Close proximity worked in your favour." She gives her a disdainful smile. Asher stiffens, his eyes flashing with anger. Emily puts her hand on top of his.

"It did. I am the luckiest girl in the world." Emily gazes at Asher with so much affection, it eases some of the tension in his body and his shoulders relax visibly.

"I have to agree with you." She touches the pearls around her neck and sighs.

We all eat in uncomfortable silence. The air around us is suffocating with negativity. I flinch when Lydia speaks again. "What was the name of the girl who barged into your penthouse unannounced?"

My jaw hardens. What is she up to? Why is she bringing up Rochelle's topic now? Her eyes glint when she sees me gripping the fork too hard.

Schooling my features, I respond. "Rochelle Moore."

Emily is the one to stiffen this time. "What? Why would she do that?" she looks at me with furrowed brows. Her protectiveness towards her sister is visible in her body language, her hackles raised.

"She is your sister, I take it?" Lydia raises her eyebrow.

"She is." Emily lifts her chin up. She was listening to Lydia throwing insults her way and didn't say a word but *one* mention of her sister and she was getting defensive. I am impressed.

"Oh, dear. Ill-mannered girls. Does it run in the family?" she wrinkles her nose in disgust.

Emily looks horrified and stunned but before she could say her piece, the loud screeching sound of the chair stops her. Asher stands. "That's it. I am done. You can't insult my girlfriend and her family. Not on my fucking watch."

"Is this the way to talk to your mother?"

"Well… you get what you give, *mother*." He spits the last word like an insult and grasps Emily's hand, pulling her up.

"I am sorry, brother but I can't do this." He strides away, leaving me alone.

I admire Asher.

I can't do what he did. One wrong move from my side can ruin the acquisition and many people's jobs are on the line. I can't let my emotions get to me.

There are no sentiments in business after all. It was easy up until now.

CHAPTER 29

Rochelle

"John," I wave at him when I see him entering the building lobby.

He approaches me. "Ms. Moore." He nods with a small smile curling his lips.

"Rochelle." I correct and he nods again. He is just like his employer. A man of few words.

"I wanted to give this to Mr. Will. Can you take this to him?" I hand him the box.

"Certainly."

"Thank you." I smile and walk out of the building.

Last night when I was coming home after helping Emily get ready, my mind was filled with questions.

The thought I tried so hard to eradicate started pestering me.

Who was I to Alan Will? I was definitely not his girlfriend. Was I just a fling? But it felt more than that. Questions like these kept me up all night.

I was also missing him. Terribly. I missed his eye-smiles.

The way he used to brush my hair aside to kiss my brow. The way he used to ask questions with his eyes alone.

I miss his scent but most of all I missed the warmth only his embrace could provide.

He is yet to contact me but that didn't stop me from baking him a cake first thing in the morning.

I knew I wasn't allowed to visit him like I used to before. I was going to drop the cake box by the reception area but I found John.

The fact that I am sending him a cake after everything might be weird.

It may make me look like a clingy girl but I wanted to do this for him.

You hurt my heart, Alan but I can't stop loving you. I'll fight for both of us. My masochist heart still belongs to you. I'll wait for you.

After returning to my apartment, I spend most of the day cleaning and doing laundry.

I eat an early light supper and settle in the living room with my laptop. It's time to browse culinary schools.

I finally find a decent program after an hour of internet surfing. They offer flexible scheduling for meeting the student's lifestyle.

I am so enthralled by their website pictures and details that the doorbell ringing doesn't register.

I glance at the wall clock. Eight p.m.

Frowning, I close the laptop and place it on the couch beside me before getting up.

The face that greets me upon opening the door makes me almost lose my footing.

"What are you doing here, Alan?"

He stares at me silently, his dark eyes taking me in.

That's when I realize I am in a plain tank top and shorts. I fold my arms across my chest. His gaze drops to my arms. Then slides back up to my face.

"You baked a cake for me." He advances, making me stumble back. He closes the door when he's inside and begins stalking me again.

"I-It was your birthday."

"After what happened, you still did it," he says softly but his steps are confident as he approaches.

My back hits the wall. With long strides, he is in my private space.

My palm connects his chest to stop him.

"If you're hinting that I am pathetic—" I forget to breathe when his chest is flush against mine.

He clutches my waist in a tight grip. I am about to shut my eyes in relief but shake myself internally.

I turn away when his lips descend. "You can't do this."

"You're mine. I can do whatever the hell I want."

I look at him. "Why are you hurting me? Don't you think we need to talk?"

His lips brush against mine. "Later."

"But—"

"You don't want me?" his intense sharp eyes search my face for an answer.

"Don't ask questions like that." I lean my head against his shoulder.

Knowing Alan, I know he wouldn't take me against my consent. I don't have the strength to fight my desire for him when he is this close to me.

I moan when he sucks on my neck. He knows that's my weak spot.

"You want me," he affirms over my lips after pulling his head back a little.

"Yes…" *I do.* It gets muffled when he crushes his lips to mine.

I lose the war between my brain and heart and submit to him. Submit to my desires.

I welcome the hot kisses and urgent touches. My tank top is pulled up and over my head. Then it's his coat jacket, shirt, and tie that adds up to the heap of clothes.

I kick the shorts when he works them down.

Alan drapes my leg around his hip.

Sliding my panties to the side, he enters me. Our hands grope each other.

With our lips fused together, he moves faster until I am exploding with so many sensations.

Alan doesn't stop. He takes me again and again like he is making up for the lost time.

Later, when we are lying on my bed tangled in each other, I start. "We need to talk."

"We do." He sighs.

"Well?" I look at him.

"I can't explain it to you. My mother is… It is complicated. All you need to know is that whatever I did was to protect you."

"It's not enough of an explanation, Alan. But I can live with that." For now.

I can't lose him. I hug him tightly and feel his lips on the crown of my head.

He wanted to protect me. Alan was looking out for me by hurting me.

It sounds weirder the more I think about it.

"I have to go."

"You're not staying?" I hate how small my voice is.

"I can't." I wait for him to explain more but he doesn't. Climbing off the bed, he heads to the living room to get his clothes.

I cover my nakedness with the sheet as I watch him get dressed. The coldness chilling my bones has nothing to do with the climate.

I didn't get to tell him about my conversation with my parents and he didn't ask.

I want to tell him everything but I feel the first wall being erected by my heart.

Not to keep him out, but to protect itself.

His hasty goodbye kiss doesn't warm me. But I still hold on because I don't want to give up on us. Not yet.

The next few days fly by completing the formalities of my culinary school. I have chosen the mid-morning program of eight months.

The decision of choosing that time slot was influenced because of Alan.

My world revolves around him. He rarely has time for me. Knowing his tight schedule, I chose the timing of 11:00 a.m. to 3 p.m.

I walk out of the building. It was my first day today and I desperately want to see Alan.

I have so much to tell him. I pull my phone out and contemplate over calling him.

What if he is in the middle of something important? My giddiness wins and I find myself hitting the call icon beside his name.

"Rochelle." He answers in that husky voice of his that escalates my heartbeats.

"Hi," what was I going to say? Oh, yes. "Alan… I wanted to ask if you are free tonight?"

"I'll be at your place at my usual time, love." Alan usually comes around seven in the evening and leaves shortly after our intense lovemaking. We never get time to talk and I want to change that.

"No… I was thinking about us having dinner at this cool place near my school."

"Rochelle." The firmness in his tone signals me what he is going to say. "Text me the name of this place. I'll get takeout on my way to yours."

My shoulders slump. "Okay."

That night when we were eating in my kitchen, I couldn't help but test the waters. "Alan…"

"Mm-hmm."

"I think we should tell our families about us."

His fork hangs mid-air at my suggestion. Setting the fork down, he dabs at his mouth with tissues.

"We can't."

"Why not?"

"Why do you want to tell them?" he tilts his head and studies me.

"Because it has been more than a month since we are seeing each other. Aren't you sick of this hiding business?"

"I can't give you what you're asking of me, Rochelle. Not right now."

I drop my gaze but he takes my chin between his fingers and tips my face up. "We don't need to do this. You're mine and nothing will change that fact."

I force my lips to smile and bury my face in his neck when he abandons the food and carries me to my bedroom.

SINFUL LOVE

That night when he leaves me in my bed alone again, I curl into my pillow and cry myself to sleep.

CHAPTER 30

Two weeks later

Rochelle

A lone tear slips from my eye as I cry out before falling back on the mattress.

Alan rests his head on my collarbone as we both lay there for a moment.

After a minute, he lifts his head and kisses me on the lips before falling beside me. His raspy breaths draw my attention.

I turn to look at him. His beautiful features are coated with perspiration from our lovemaking.

Stealing a few minutes for my own, I watch as his breathing steadies. I curl my fingers to stop myself from touching him.

Pressure building under my lids forces me to get up. I feel the weight of his gaze on my back as I close the bathroom door behind me.

I grip the vanity as I dare to look at my reflection.

My cheeks are flushed, my lips are swollen from his drugging kisses, and my hair is a mess from his fingers.

It is my eyes staring back at me that cements my decision.

The once expressive eyes are now oddly emotionless. I have to do this for myself.

I said I wouldn't give up on us but my resolve couldn't even last for two weeks.

In the period of fourteen days, he made time to visit me every day for two hours. And that hours were spent in silence while our bodies talked to each other.

Mine was begging him to stay another minute and his body conveyed the frustration of the circumstances he was in.

Countless times, I tried talking to him but he always had something important that needed him more than I did.

He may think spending two hours between the sheets would keep me satisfied but he was unaware that it was slowly draining me out of the happiness I once felt with him.

I couldn't help but feel like his dirty little secret. One that he was hiding behind closed doors. While he claimed that he was doing all this to protect me, his actions were hurting me more.

While Alan always satisfied me sexually, it was him that I craved more. His company, his scent when I used to bury my nose in his shirt, shared dinners.

Sex wasn't enough.

I am slowly turning into a doormat. I am beginning to hate this weaker version of me and before I direct that hate toward him, I need to end this.

After cleaning up, I pull the robe from the bathroom rack and cover my nakedness.

The bathroom door opens and Alan's reflection appears in the mirror behind me. He still manages to steal my breath away with a single glance.

I smile at him even though I can hear the cracking of my heart.

Don't do this. My heart begs me.

I have to. I mourn.

"Close your eyes." His front brushes against my back. He is fully dressed now which means he is going to leave soon.

Without questions, I obey him one last time and close my eyes.

I feel a delicate graze around my neck.

Alan sweeps my hair out of the way and a minute later I feel his hot breath over my ear as he speaks, "Now slowly open your eyes."

I gasp, my fingers reach up to touch the heart-shaped emerald pendant with the round diamond set on top. The delicate white-gold chain is so thin yet it suffocates me.

"Do you like it?" he kisses the shell of my ear.

"It's beautiful." I choke out. "But I can't accept it." He catches my hand when I try to reach for the clasp of the necklace.

"You are keeping it. End of discussion." He turns me around. "Now give me a kiss before I leave." He lowers his head to kiss me but I turn my head to the side and his lips connect my cheek.

"Let's end it." I close my eyes, asking the universe to grant me enough strength to mask the pain my own words caused.

Alan tenses. His heat leaves me as he takes a few steps back. "Look at me when you talk." His cold voice makes me look at him, shivering when his eyes bore into me.

Despite his cold demeanor, I can still notice his stiffened shoulders.

"I can't do this anymore," I speak softly and gesture between the two of us.

"Why?" he asks with such tenderness, it breaks my heart. I close my eyes for a minute to compose myself before answering.

"I want more…" I lift a shoulder in a shrug while biting my lip, my chin trembling. "I want to hold your hand in public. I want the right to hug you and kiss you in front of our friends and family…." A tear slips. "I want to spend time with you outside of my bedroom, Alan. I want respect."

He strides to me and cups my face in his hands. "Have I ever disrespected you?"

"Verbally no but your actions make me feel like I am your mistress… and then you are gifting me expensive jewelry… I wanted you, Alan… only you. Nowadays, you don't even have time to ask me how my day was. All this time, I tried to figure out what kind of "relationship we had. I thought we were more than a fling. I thought what we had was more than an affair. But I am not so sure anymore. What are we to each other?"

"A label can't define what we have." He grits out.

"What *do* we have, Alan?" I remove his hand from my face and pad out of the bathroom with him hot on my heels.

I hug my middle as I stop at the other end of my bedroom.

"Rochelle?"

I turn to face him. "I love you, Alan. So much, it hurts me…. here." I rub the left side of my chest. "I can't be your sexual partner anymore… it was my stupidity to think we are more than this… that *I* am more than this for you."

He grips my shoulders and backs me up against the wall. "You are."

He towers over me, his darkened eyes raking over my features like he can't get enough of looking at me.

I tremble in his hold and my breathing becomes ragged. That's how much he affects me.

I push at his chest hard. It takes him by surprise and he staggers back, hurt flash in his eyes.

"Don't lie to me." I whimper.

"I am not, Rochelle. You have to understand…"

"Make me understand then. Enlighten me. Why do you hesitate upon being seen with me? Why did you refuse when I suggested going out for dinner?"

"I was protecting you." He shouts.

"You keep saying that," I murmur.

"I am ready to tell you everything if that's what it takes to make you understand."

"It doesn't matter anymore!" I shout and break into sobs. "You don't even love me," I shake my head in dismay.

"I love you, goddammit!" he jerks me to his chest, his lips a centimeter away from me.

"You are saying that out of fear of losing me. I have become your habit. But don't worry, you'll get over it with time." Numbness spreads over me as I speak.

"I fell for you the moment my eyes landed on you in that café three months ago." His eyes flare with an emotion I can't recognize.

I am close to breaking. So close to taking him in my arms and begging him to forget about this fight.

But then, I remember all the times he didn't say those three words back. "Why didn't you say it back when I confessed my love for you?"

"I wasn't aware how deeper my feelings were for you at that time, Rochelle. I didn't want to give you empty words. That's not me."

"Whatever you tell me now won't change how awful the past two weeks have been for me. I can't live like this. Miserable and alone."

"You're not alone."

I just give him a sad smile. "I want you to leave." It pains me so much to say it but I need to do this for myself.

Alan hesitates for a few beats before letting his hands fall to his sides.

I turn around when he starts toward the door. Just because I asked him to leave doesn't mean I have the strength to watch him go.

His footsteps stop and I could feel his eyes on my back.

"I am going for now because I respect your wishes, Rochelle. But don't even for a second think that this is over. We are far from over. I'll prove my love to you."

With that, he walks out of my apartment and… my life.

CHAPTER 31

Rochelle

I wake up early the next day despite sleeping for only a couple of hours.

I fix a bowl of oatmeal for breakfast before getting ready for my class, my actions pure mechanical.

The thrill I used to get after waking up knowing I am going to spend my day doing something I love—cooking—is missing in action.

A part-time job would be good for me. It would help me in distracting myself during idle hours and the money wouldn't hurt.

SINFUL LOVE

Alan was kind enough to pay me for the internship but it's time for job hunting.

I grow still at his reminder. Every time I do something, no matter what it is, my brain somehow conjures up things that connect with Alan.

Like my hair tie reminds me of the way he used to pull it off to free my hair. Not even twenty-four hours without him and I am struggling to exist in my own house.

My heart is silent today. There are no whines from it. I know why.

Because Alan walked out from my apartment last night with it in his unforgiving grip. Or maybe it was my heart that was desperately clinging to him.

Alan is my first love and I would never be able to love someone else again.

I do not regret my time with him but I was tired of fighting. I wanted to be fought for. He decided to fight for us but it was too late.

I was settling for the bread crumbs he was providing when I deserved more than that.

I was terrified of losing him. Yet, I had to end things with him because sometimes the hardest things you do turn out to be right for you in the long run.

The worst battle was over. I have to collect the remaining pieces of me so I could build myself up again.

I put on the tan coat over my plain white tee and denim. After I have my suede ankle boots on, I grab my baby pink backpack and head for the door.

My eyes drop to the bouquet of burgundy roses on my doorstep.

Sinking to my knees I touch the delicate flowers with my fingertips. The feel of the velvety soft petals along with the dark color of the roses is mesmerizing.

Something prickles my fingers in the mass of silkiness and I pluck it.

A card.

A handwritten card. My eyes jump down to read my favorite name in the world.

The butterflies I feel in my stomach are untamable. The tickles make me feel alive again.

I sit on my heels and inhale air that is laced with roses *he* sent. Then I read…

Have a great day at school, Rochelle.

I love you.

Alan.

I trace his sharp and bold handwriting, my fingers stopping at those words.

Why can't I believe you? I got what I wanted. He said those three words. Yet it feels untrue.

Standing up, I take the roses back inside and place them on the kitchen counter. Don't make it harder for me, Alan. Don't. I whisper to the flowers as if they could convey my message to him. Giving the bouquet one last look, I leave the apartment.

Throughout the day my mind keeps flashing his handwritten card. All the pep talk I gave myself went out the window when I read his message.

For so long I was pretending to be okay that now I am unsure of how to feel anymore.

A cool breeze caresses my face as I step out of the premises.

A girl from my class waves me before she heads to the right, quickly disappearing into the crowd of the sidewalk.

I turn the other direction, not in the mood to head to the empty apartment so soon.

I freeze when my eyes catch a glimpse of a tall figure in a black suit. He has his back turned to me.

I duck behind a pillar of the building when he turns my way. What is Alan doing here?

Out of the corner of my eye, I notice a few girls sneaking intrigued glances at him.

I grit my teeth when the group of girls giggle, still ogling my Alan.

He is not yours, Rochelle.

I shouldn't do this. I find myself shuffling to the edge of the pillar.

One peek. I just need one little glimpse of him before I go home.

Before I could stop myself, my head is leaning to the right, my head craning to get a proper look at him without being caught in the act.

He moves and I get to stare at his gorgeous profile.

He once said to never give up on my dreams. I have everything now except for him.

Alan is that one dream of mine that will never see fulfillment.

The plan of aimlessly roaming the city fails and I find myself back in my apartment.

I pick one of my favorite romance novels and curl in my lounge chair. Reading is an escape for me.

The book provides me its companionship until there is darkness outside and my stomach is grumbling from lack of food.

Setting the book on the coffee table, I stretch my limbs. I pick the phone and head to the kitchen.

Unlocking the phone, my breath hitches for the third time in the day.

He texted me. Around noon.

My thumb moves back and forth in contemplation before touching on the notification.

You looked beautiful today. Good night, baby. I love you.

My heart is pounding hard. He saw me. I read his message again and again. My vision gets blurry and I realize I am crying.

The next day is a repeat of yesterday.

The lack of sleep is making me feel cranky, the fatigue slowing my movements.

When I open the door, I was half-expecting another bouquet but the sight before me almost makes me fall. I grip the door for balance.

"Alan…" I forget how to breathe.

He is in yet another custom-made suit. And although his appearance is impeccable like always, it's his eyes that give him away.

His sleep-deprived gaze matches my own. Has he been working all night?

Why is he here during his work hours?

His eyes sweep over me, taking in my ponytail that's touching my blush color peacoat.

"What are you doing here, Alan?" I drop my eyes to his shoes.

"I want to talk to you."

I swallow hard, hearing his deep voice is making me emotional.

"There's nothing left to talk." My voice is weak. "I am sorry I have to go." I lock the door with shaky hands and sidestep him to walk away.

I feel like I am going to collapse.

I cried the entire way to school, sat through classes with swollen eyes and a splitting headache.

Why can't he leave me alone? He can't give me what I want and I won't settle for less.

The reason I am refusing to talk to him is that I know myself. I *will* take him back in a heartbeat and the suffering will begin all over again.

I will never go back to how things were.

I am dragging my feet toward my apartment, the longing for the comfort of my bed increasing with every step.

My tired legs cause a misstep and I yelp.

Strong arms sweep me up. The wind chooses the correct time to breeze past us. I breathe in his familiar scent.

Alan's eyes lock on mine.

"Are you all right?" He asks in a worried voice. What is he doing here? His suit is a bit rumpled, as is his hair.

"You came back?" I whisper.

"I never left." He says in a grave voice.

"Oh, Alan." My hand reaches up to cup his jaw but I stop before I could touch him. He can't do this to me. He knows how much he affects me and is using it against me. Hardening my heart, I jerk out of his hold.

"Leave, please."

"Will you talk to me?"

"No."

"Then I am not going anywhere." His face is solemn.

"Suit yourself." I move past him and slam the door shut after I get inside.

Sliding down the door, I bring my knees to my chest and hug them before breaking into sobs.

Alan continued showing up every day and it was taking a toll on me. Every day his actions were piercing my defenses.

I sat and sobbed every night in the crumbling ruins of the walls I had built around my heart to protect it.

In each card I found in the bouquets he left at my doorstep every morning and the nightly text messages, he never failed to write *I love you.*

I won't be appeased with that. Either he is all in with me or he has to remain completely out of my life.

Today marks the twelfth day since we broke up.

A new day but I know there would be nothing new. I'll open the door and find him waiting. And if he is not there, his bouquet would be. I'll ignore him like it doesn't affect me in the least and head to my class.

When I open the door there's no sign of Alan. I look down. No flowers either.

Did he give up on me already? I sound like a hypocrite. I should be relieved he finally stopped showing up. I should be but I am not.

After my last class, I head straight home. I needed to buy groceries but for some reason, I was expecting to see him outside my apartment. He wasn't there.

Not seeing him all day fills me with irrational thoughts and worry.

I think of calling him to know whether he is okay but stop myself. What if he *chose* not to come? That'll make me look like a fool.

I immerse myself in cleaning the apartment. Again. It helps me from having a meltdown. It keeps me busy. I can't even read now as it amplifies what I am missing. So, cleaning it is.

I flop on my couch after I am done. Then I remember I had to buy groceries.

Groaning, I get up and fetch my purse.

With sacks of groceries, I exit the store and start toward my apartment.

I regret carrying an umbrella with me. The sky was cloudy and I didn't want to be drenched in rain. Now I have to carry the weight of it along with the sacks.

Halfway through, I feel the first droplet of water on my cheek and in a minute, it starts raining.

I look for a place to take shelter. Rushing across the street, I stand under the front shade of a bakery.

Placing the sacks down, I open the umbrella. I pick up the sacks and resume walking.

My skin prickles with awareness of being watched when I turn the corner of my block. My heart begins to race. It halts my feet and I turn my head left then right.

Nobody in particular stands out among the people passing by.

Shrugging, I start again but the feeling is stronger now.

Without thinking, I turn on my heels and freeze. Standing a few feet away from me is Alan.

My eyes take in his white button-down shirt which is now drenched by the rain.

Without giving it much thought, I run to him and hold the umbrella over both of us.

He reads the unspoken question in my eyes and gives me a tired smile. "I was swamped with work today. I came to you the moment I could."

"You're all wet," I murmur.

Because of me.

His eyes drop to my chest which causes me to look down at myself.

Just a few minutes in rain and my thin tank top is now clinging to my breasts like a second skin.

He knows I caught him checking me out just now but rather than appearing sheepish, his face is unapologetic.

I clear my throat. "Where are you parked?"

"Outside your building."

How did I not see it? Maybe I didn't look for his car because he didn't show up the entire day.

"Let's go," I tell him. He nods and takes the sacks from my hand. I open my mouth to object but my protests die down with his single glare.

We walk in silence. The constant brushing of his arm against mine makes my already racing heart pound faster.

We stop once we reach his sleek car. "Go home, Alan."

"Are you willing to hear me out?"

I shake my head. A muscle clenches in his jaw.

"Then I guess I'll wait for you like usual."

My instincts order me to take him inside the apartment. But I ignore it.

Taking the bags from his hands, I walk away from him. Again.

My act of toughness doesn't even last for five minutes. I curse and grab the umbrella again.

I march out and find him right where I left him. He's looking straight at me like he expected me to come out.

"This is madness," I mutter and cross the road to reach him.

Without making eye contact, I reach for his hand and close it around the handle of the umbrella.

Grasping his other hand, I drop the one thing that kept me connected to him.

His eyes fall on the emerald necklace in his hand before snapping up.

Subconsciously, I knew returning this gift would mean slashing all the ties I have with him for good.

I was going to return it to him eventually but held out till now. Why? I don't know. Maybe because returning it to him would be final.

I would have no excuses left to ever see him again.

He realizes the same because his eyes shine with understanding and for the first time, he looks vulnerable.

With his disheveled clothes and wet hair, Alan Will looks like he has truly lost for the first time in his life.

CHAPTER 32

Rochelle

Mason and Lucas got married today.

It's scary how time changes everything. It feels like only yesterday when we were here in Los Angeles for Mason's engagement party when in reality it was a little over a month ago.

During that trip, I confessed my love to Alan. And today, we are no longer together.

But time failed to change my feelings. Alan stopped coming after I gave him the neckless two days ago.

He finally listened and stopped. He didn't even accompany us on the private jet. His decision was influenced by me, I know.

Throughout the ceremony, I kept glancing around the banquet hall but couldn't find him. I did see someone who resembled his physique, but couldn't see his face.

Emily and Serah cried like babies as the couple exchanged their vows.

Asher being a doting boyfriend, had a box of tissues ready for Em. And it was sweet to watch Tatum caressing Serah's baby bump gently to soothe her.

Now the newlyweds are heading outside for wedding pictures with their friends and family.

Emily loops her arm with mine and practically drags me outside to the grand staircase.

"Come on, Rochelle. It'll be fun!"

I notice that the photographer is only selecting couples to stand on the stairs. I turn to tell her so but words abandon me.

Standing not a few feet away from me is that same tall figure in a tuxedo I had seen earlier in the hall. I don't even have to take another step to know it's him. Alan is engrossed in a conversation with Asher and Tatum.

"What's up with you?" Emily asks. I notice rather too late that she followed the line of my sight.

She is right in wondering why I am suddenly staring at Alan. Guilt pierces my heart.

My sister doesn't have a single clue what has been happening in my life.

"N-nothing. I'm just feeling a little out of place with all the make-up and the dress." I motion at my rose-gold dress and the loose curls in my hair and the make-up Emily helped me with.

She is still looking at me with narrowed eyes when Lucas claps his hands together, "Okay, guys pair up!"

I am grateful she drops the topic and follows the photographer's directions.

In a few minutes, all the couples are positioned on the stairs.

Lucas and Mason take the center spot of the entryway. Tatum and Serah are standing on the left side and Asher and Emily take the right corner.

Lucas's sister and her husband are seated on the third step.

The photographer is really talented. With few directions, he had them all posing like models.

I sneak a glance at Alan who's now standing at the far corner of the staircase to avoid coming into the frame.

I notice with disappointment that he hasn't glanced my way. Not once.

Even now, he is observing everyone except for me. Like I am invisible to his eyes.

"We need one more couple to go over there." The photographer calls out and points at the space opposite Lucas's sister.

"Rochelle, honey, what are you doing there?" Come here." Lucas waves at me to join them.

I bite my lower lip hard as pain courses through me. Who am I going to pose with? Unlike them, I have no one. No companion.

I swallow the lump in my throat. "Umm, this is a couples' only photo. I'll sit this one out." I force a smile.

It is better if I hide somewhere for a while. It is not fair to the couple to have a sulking girl around and spoiling their day. I am about to head back inside the hall when a hand slides around my waist.

My eyes travel up. "Alan…" I whisper.

My voice was so small I doubt he heard it. He says nothing as he ushers me forward.

He strides toward the empty spot. I can't help but walk faster to keep up with his pace.

The photographer asks Alan to hold my right hand in his as his left-hand stays wrapped around my waist.

My hand is clammy in his clasp. He draws closer and I feel the tip of his nose at my temple.

Alan inhales deeply as if he's breathing me in. "I missed you."

"And I, you," I whisper and close my eyes for a second.

Somewhere inside of me, I knew, he would be here tonight. When he was nowhere to be seen I was distraught. And when I did see him, he acted as if he doesn't know me. The emotions got the best of me and I confessed that I miss him. But doesn't he get it? His cold behavior in the company of our friends and family is what drew me away in the first place.

"Please forgive me, baby."

"I-I…." I stare up at him. He looks devastatingly handsome.

His jaw is covered by days of stubble. It gives him a rough look. I wasn't prepared for his touch and it shows with how my body is shivering.

My resistance is splintering and I need to do something. Fast.

The photographer clicks a few shots. And during every click, Alan and I were peering into each other's eyes.

He is devouring me with his eyes and it's admiring how my legs haven't given up on me. His touches and his nearness are too much.

"That was excellent. Thank you, guys." The photographer says and that's my cue to escape. I squirm free and climb up the stairs to head inside.

After the first dance, all the guests went to join the newlyweds on the dance floor.

I am sitting at the table by myself. I chuckle when Emily stamps on Asher's feet a couple of times while dancing.

She was always fond of dancing and is good at it so her stamping on his feet seems deliberate.

I look away when Asher pulls her against his chest and starts grinding.

Lucas is no different. Mason is grinning from ear to ear as Lucas uses him as a pole to dance.

I smile as I survey the room. My smile wipes off as my eyes stop on him.

Alan is standing across the hall with a group of men, watching me.

He wants me. It is apparent and I want him just as much… or maybe more.

Wanting each other doesn't mean we want the same things. He refuses to give me what I want and I refuse to become what he wants me to be.

At this point, I am not even sure what he wants. His apology seems genuine but he still can't accept me publicly.

I can't stop comparing my situation with my friends.

Suppose I patch things up with Alan, what then? Would we go back to having quickies in the bathroom and later acting like we don't know each other? I can't spend my life hoping and waiting for him to do the things I expect of him.

Manipulating him into doing so would also be unfair. I seem to be walking on a path with no destination.

Alan excuses himself and strides to the open doors of the hall. I notice that he has a phone to his ear.

Who is he talking to? My eyes follow him until he is out of sight. Where did he go? Is he leaving already?

My phone slips away from my fidgety hands and falls on the carpet.

After today, I won't ever get to see him again. This was it. I blink away the tears before bending down to pick it up. My hand brushes against someone else's.

"Allow me." Baby blue eyes meet me and my eyebrows jump up in surprise to find Raleigh Jackson on his haunches.

"Raleigh,"

He grins. "You remember me."

He grabs my phone and rises to his feet effortlessly. I take the phone from his extended hand.

"May I?" he motions to the empty seat at my table, still grinning. He looks dapper in a fitted tux.

"Please," I say softly but the thickness in my voice betrays me.

"I am not going to ask you if you're okay. First, because it's a lame question. And second, you'd give a one-word answer that would ramp up the awkward silence." He says as he takes the seat.

I chuckle before sniffling. "You're pretty insightful on this topic."

He shrugs, giving me a lazy smile. But then he turns serious. "Do you wanna talk about whatever's bothering you? My friends say I am a pretty good listener."

"I'm sure you are." I smile. "But I don't want to talk about it."

"Okay." He cocks his head to the side and examines me. "Why did you look surprised on seeing me?"

"Because I didn't see you up until now."

"Ouch." He moans, clutching his heart as if he took an arrow straight to his chest. "And here I had eyes only for you." He sighs dramatically.

"Uh…" I give him a bashful smile as words elude my brain.

"I am wounded, Elle." He feigns a wince and shakes his head at me.

Did he just call me Elle?

He looks like he's joking but what if I genuinely hurt him?

"I am sorry, I—"

"Dance with me."

He changes his expressions so fast it takes me by surprise. This man is so unpredictable.

"What?" I squeak.

"You know… dancing where two people move rhythmically to music." He raises his eyebrow mockingly.

"I don't dance," I murmur, giving him a sheepish smile.

In a matter of few minutes, Raleigh not only stopped me from bursting into tears, but he also made me smile.

What's surprising is he did it without any hassle.

"Consider it for my comfort and… what's the term called? Ah, a consolation prize of some sort."

"Huh?"

"You wounded my heart. I have scars to prove it. You don't believe me? let me show you." He reaches up to unbutton his coat jacket and I raise my palms up.

"I'll dance with you!"

"Good," he smirks and gives me his hand to take.

"You're evil, you know that?" I huff and place my hand in his.

"I've been called worse. By my archenemy." He mumbles the last part and stands.

Grabbing my hand, he leads me to the dance floor.

The DJ is playing a slow number. Raleigh pulls me close with a hand at the small of my back.

With one hand in his and the other on his chest, we start to move.

Raleigh keeps respectable space between our bodies, giving me one more reason to like him.

"Archenemy?" I ask because for some reason I can't picture someone hating him to the point of being his archenemy. And also because I am in desperate need of a distraction.

"Yeah. Her name's Hannah." He sighs.

"A girl." I prompt.

"She's my co-worker who doesn't miss a single opportunity to piss me the fuck off."

"Oh, how do you deal with it then?"

The corner of his mouth curves in a sinister smirk. "I always find ways to make her life difficult."

My eyebrows shoot up. He sounds like he enjoys this rivalry with his opponent.

"Now it's your turn."

"My turn to do what?" I look up at him. He's so tall. I barely reach his chin.

"I answered your questions, now you answer mine. Why are you upset?"

"I am not." I shake my head. He only blinks at me.

"You're the only girl who's sitting all alone while your friends are dancing and having fun. There are only two reasons why a beautiful girl like you appears heartbroken at someone's wedding.

"One, if the *groom* is your ex—which is next to impossible as Lucas is gay. And two, when someone on the guest list is your ex. My money is on the latter."

I stare at him, my mouth agape.

"I am a genius." He chuckles.

"Indeed," I murmur and he sobers up.

"Name the asshole who broke your heart, Elle. I can beat the shit out of him for you." His protectiveness gives me a brotherly vibe from him.

Alan might've hurt me but I can never wish him harm, even if Raleigh means it as a joke.

"That's sweet of you to say but it wouldn't fill the emptiness in my life now, would it?" My wobbly chin drops to my chest.

"Fuck." He tries to look at me by bending his head. "Don't cry, please."

He mutters another curse. "Who hurt you like that?"

I have been suffering in agony for so long with no one to share my feelings with. So when Raleigh asks me again, I don't hold back.

I tell him everything but exclude telling him Alan's name.

From how I fell in love at first sight to how I broke things off two weeks ago.

He patiently listens to me as I tell him how I died little by little every day I had to slam my

door at his face. And I confess with shame how
much I want him back regardless of my self-
respect.

"This guy loves you, Elle. But I get your
dilemma. What if he has his reasons for hiding the
relationship?"

"If he really did love me, then nothing else
should matter. He has always been my priority.
Why's my expecting the same in return so
wrong?" I want to weep but I hold it in by biting
my lip.

"It's not. But I can speak with certainty that he
does love you."

"He doesn't," I mumble.

Raleigh's gaze drifts behind me for a few
seconds in contemplation before bringing his baby
blue eyes back to me. "Let's find out."

He bends down, his lips awfully close to mine.
Tilting my head back, I squeak, "What are you
doing?!"

"It's showtime."

"What?!"

"You're like a sister to me but I—" A hand
springs from the side and I gape, horrified as
Raleigh is pulled off me by his collar in one hard
yank. He stumbles few steps back.

I turn my head to find Alan stalking toward
Raleigh.

"Hey, man. What's your problem? Can't you see I was having a good time—" Alan slams his fist in Raleigh's face.

For several seconds, the silence continues before I hear gasps of disbelief.

The guests converse in whispers and I stand there in shock, unable to think what to do next.

Alan punched Raleigh. Alan wasn't a violent person.

The sight of blood oozing from Raleigh's lower lip dwindles my shock.

I spring to action and get between them.

Pushing on Alan's chest, I try to put some distance between the two. His rage terrifies me. He is not looking at me. His entire focus is fixed on the man behind me who has not backed away from his spot.

What is wrong with Raleigh? Why did he provoke Alan by saying things like that? I can't think about that right now.

He starts pushing me aside, trying to lunge at him again. "Alan! no…" I slide my hands up and down his chest to calm him when my own heart was pounding.

Our friends approach us and I hear them asking Raleigh if he's okay.

I keep my eyes trained on Alan, my hands not leaving him even for a second.

"What the fuck, Alan? Why did you do that?" I hear Asher's voice.

I notice that the music has stopped and the murmurs are becoming louder among the people surrounding us.

At his brother's question, Alan's gaze falls on me. His eyes blaze with heat. "He dared to touch what was mine."

My mouth goes dry. I can't believe he said that out loud. He is acting like he doesn't care about people knowing about us anymore. Is he the same man who said he couldn't give me what I wanted?

I don't allow myself to be happy, not yet.

"My work here is done." All eyes pivot in Raleigh's direction.

Silence.

Not a soul speaks and the murmurs stop.

Raleigh wipes the blood off the corner of his lip with a thumb. He winks at me.

His lips kick up into a smirk as he moves past me.

I turn to watch him and so do others, the crowd dividing in two automatically for him to pass.

He grabs a flute of sparkling champagne from a waiter's tray on his way and raises it.

"Cheers," he takes a sip and leaves the hall.

Now I understand the motive behind his actions.

He proved to me that Alan does love me. He took a punch and gave me the proof in return that Alan cares.

Provoked by Raleigh, Alan took a stand for me. For us.

But, wait? How did Raleigh guess the man I was talking about was Alan? What boggles me more is the fact that without me disclosing Alan's identity, Raleigh figured it out and he executed the whole act with excellence.

Emily chooses that moment to speak. "Do I have to ask, or you could read my mind? What the hell is going on between you two?" she grabs my arm and pulls me away from Alan.

She is not my sister anymore because she has slipped into the role of a mother-hen now. She doesn't realize that I am an adult and soon going to turn nineteen. For her, I am her baby sister, her kiddo.

Emily's question draws the attention of others and I flush with embarrassment.

Alan doesn't let her create space between us and clutches my other hand and drags me back toward him. "Emily, you can ask these questions in private. There's no need to discuss it when we have an audience."

She narrows her eyes. "Who are you to tell me how and when to talk to my sister?"

He wraps a possessive hand around my waist. "Her boyfriend."

Alan

Rochelle's beautiful forest green eyes fly up to me.

Her disbelief-filled gaze shatters me. I was so caught up in work that I kept hurting the one I can't live without. It was unfair of me to prioritize my work, my relationship with my mother more than her.

I thought that if I could hide my relationship with Rochelle, it would appease Lydia.

Growing up, I have witnessed Lydia ruining people's lives for lesser offenses. Being one of the powerful families in the world gives you advantages.

One phone call from her can ruin your life. One moment you are living a peaceful life, the other your life is in shambles.

I have seen numerous people losing their jobs, even being forced to relocate because of her.

I didn't want Rochelle to live that fate. It was highly possible of her to use Rochelle against me.

She expressed her objection to the changes in the acquisition plan.

Had she known about me and Rochelle, she wouldn't have hesitated to use it to force my hand.

In the whirlwind of what-ifs, I lost Rochelle.

She was the only good thing in my life. When she left me, I realised—rather too late—that I don't want a billion-dollar deal if it costs me my Rochelle.

Nothing and no one else in this world matter to me. Except for the girl staring at me right now.

"I don't know the first thing about love but here I am, loving your sister anyway. With everything in me." I speak to Emily but my entire attention is on Rochelle.

My heart skips a beat when she looks at me with tears in her eyes.

For the first time in two weeks, she is letting me see her real self again.

Every time she slammed the door in my face, I could see she was putting a brave front to appear uncaring.

But she cared, didn't she?

This girl was filled with so much compassion and love that she was brimming with it.

I scan the faces around me. The room is silent. They're all staring at me with their mouths hanging open and rightfully so.

It is shocking for them to find out about us but what makes it even more jarring is the way it came out.

I was drunk on jealousy. What I did with Raleigh was not me.

It was a man who wanted to claim what was his. I was blinded with rage and couldn't see that Raleigh was provoking me.

When I finished the important call and returned inside, what I saw boiled my blood. When Raleigh leaned down to kiss her, I snapped.

I didn't give much thought that I was ruining someone's big day.

I just wanted him off of her. He said his work here was done.

That meant he had figured out what was happening between me and Rochelle.

In a fucked up way, he got to me and made me talk. It is fucked up because he put himself at risk tonight by pulling that stunt.

And for what? To reunite me and Rochelle? He might be a good man but a cocky bastard at that.

I was going to tell everyone about us later today but not like this.

Guilt washes over me. I have no right to stay after what I did.

Reluctantly, I step away from her, my hand feeling the loss of Rochelle's warmth.

"Please, forgive me." I regard the married couple with my sincere gaze and turn to leave.

I stare at Rochelle one last time before exiting the banquet hall.

CHAPTER 33

Rochelle

That infuriating man left. Without me.

How can he just leave after saying things like that? Didn't he know I was pushing him away for the last two weeks in the hopes of *him* pulling me closer?

My feet want to go after him. I don't believe in soulmates but I know what I have with him is rare and I'd be stupid to let it go.

He is my first love. My first kiss. My first heartbreak. My first everything. And I want him to be my last everything.

SANJANA NIDHI

I look to my side when Emily intertwines our fingers, a soft look of understanding mixed with hurt in her eyes. "Why didn't you tell me, kiddo?"

"I'm sorry." Tears sting my eyes. She pulls me into a hug and I squeeze her tight. "I love him. So much."

She strokes my hair gently. "I know." Her voice is so gentle like she understands what I am going through.

I pull back and approach Mason and Lucas.

"I am so sorry about what happened—"

"Are you kidding me? Raleigh is my bestie. I know him. He'll be fine. But I had no idea how romantic Alan is! The way he staked a claim on you was so hot! You lucky biatch!" Lucas grins at me.

My face heats up and I turn to Mason to apologize.

"Mason…" He places a finger against my lips before hugging me.

Turning back to Emily, I say, "I have to find him. I can't let him go, Em. He is my whole life."

"First promise me that you'll tell me *everything* once we're back in New York," she raises a brow, a smile playing on her lips.

I chuckle. "I promise."

Asher comes forward. "Let me drive you to the hotel."

I shake my head. "I want to do this on my own. But thanks." I smile before running toward the exit.

Love isn't perfect. Relationships aren't easy. But if you're willing to stick together and make it work, nothing can come in the way of your happy ending.

Alan never gave up on me. He fought for us.

It doesn't mean everything's going to be easy. We'll have to work to make our love stronger. I am ready to work hard. I am ready to forget all the reasons that broke us and I am going to cling to that one reason why we could work. *Love*.

It's around eight in the evening. I have no idea where he is.

I walk through the meticulously manicured garden that leads to the parking lot. I walk between the cars and look for him.

I retrieve my phone from my clutch and scroll through the contact list and find his name. I hit call.

The sound of the phone ringing makes me turn on my heels.

Alan steps forward from behind a car, the phone still ringing in his right hand.

The relief unleashes within me and it brings tears to my eyes. I lower the phone.

"Looking for me?" he asks hoarsely, and I see vulnerability in his eyes.

I give him a shaky nod, my throat thick with emotions.

Alan pockets his phone. Slowly, Alan holds his arms out, handing me the control again. I run the short distance and throw myself at him.

He catches me, gathering me in his waiting arms.

My feet dangle a few inches above the ground, my frame molding against his. His hands are curled tightly against my waist and back, crushing me to his body.

"I love you." He pulls his head back a little.

Receiving handwritten cards and messages with these words didn't make it real until now.

This is what I have been yearning for so long.

Giving my heart to Alan Will was never planned. It happened on one sunny day when he saved me from a pissed-off customer at the café. I feel grateful to that lady and to every other thing that played a role in bringing us together.

All he had to do was save me from falling that day and I was his forever. The distance between us only made me love him harder. I won't let him go. Ever.

"I love you more," I sniffle before smiling.

"I am so sorry—"

I plant a soft kiss on his lips, rendering him silent. "I forgive you."

Placing me down on my feet, Alan cups my face with his calloused hands. His eyes darken. "I am going to tell you everything on our way back home. But first, let me kiss you right."

He bends down and kisses me until I am breathless and my heart full of joy.

That night, Alan and I left for New York.

When I asked him the reason behind his hurry, all he said was to trust him.

Even after traveling in first class, I was drained physically and emotionally. Alan drove us to his penthouse.

In the wee hours, we cuddled and passed out due to exhaustion.

The next day he woke me up early in the morning and asked me to get ready. Again, at my questioning eyes, he said, "Just trust me, love".

"What are we doing here?" I ask as we walk into the beautiful lobby of the Four Seasons Hotel.

"My mother is staying here."

His answer leaves my stomach in a knot. He had explained his equation with his mother and why he had to do what he did with me.

While I understood his reasoning, I am nowhere near ready to meet his mother.

I am already feeling out of place as is. I don't want to face her disdainful gaze.

At my hesitation, he brings our clasped hands up and kisses my fingers. "I need to do this. And I want you by my side."

I can never say no to this man. "Okay." I smile and he smiles back.

A cold feeling stirs at the pit of my stomach as we ride the elevator in silence.

I try to focus on his thumb that's brushing back and forth against my knuckles.

When we reach the presidential suite on the fifty-second floor, I am a bundle of nerves. I try to calm myself when Alan pulls out the key card.

"Is it okay to enter? I mean..." I trail. I still remember how Lydia commented upon seeing me for the first time.

She didn't know about me and Alan back then so I could give her the benefit of doubt. But when Emily told me about the dinner and how Lydia insulted us and our family, it made me believe that this woman looks down on everyone who doesn't come from money.

"She is expecting me. This meeting was arranged days ago."

"I don't understand…"

"You will once we are inside. Now come." He pushes the door open and holds it for me to enter first.

I have never seen a hotel room this huge. We walk through the narrow foyer and enter the living area. The ceiling of the room is so high I have to crane my neck.

Wait, is that a piano to the right? Why would someone need a piano in a hotel suite?

I must've said that out loud because Alan leans in. "You get a trained pianist who will come here on call whenever you want. It comes in the package. A dedicated team of people at your service."

Wow. I can never see myself living like this. The place screams money, power, and luxury, each of which I have little to no desire for.

"Alan, dear, I hope I didn't keep you waiting too long."

Lydia Will walks through a door to the far end of the living room.

She hasn't seen me yet as her focus is on the phone in her hand. She looks up and smiles at her son and as if in slow motion I witness her smile wilting the moment her eyes land on me.

She regards me with open contempt before redirecting her gaze to Alan.

"You flew me back here to New York saying you had something important to discuss that couldn't wait and then you show up with *her*." She glares at our joined hands. "What do I make out of this?"

"I hope you are having a pleasant stay, mum." His sarcastic tone makes it hard to make out whether he is actually asking her about the stay or is hinting at something else.

Lydia's eyes snap up, and she visibly tenses. In a blink, her back straightens and her lips tilt up in a tight smile. "I am, yes. Why don't you sit down and I'll ring the butler?"

"That's not necessary as this won't take long," Alan says in a calm voice.

"Nonsense. You should spend some time with your mother."

It's like I am watching a soap opera where two actors are playing a role of a mother and a son. The atmosphere feels stiff and strained as if they are strangers.

"If you did want to spend time with me you could've stayed the last time. But you were out the door the minute you realised I wasn't backing out of the acquisition like you demanded.

"And the only reason you're standing here is because I am paying fifty thousand dollars a night for this presidential suite. So why don't we get to the point and save the half-arsed attempts to make small talks?"

A gasp pierces the silence that follows Alan's response and I realize it came from me.

I am shocked by how calm he sounded the entire time he spoke to his mother. His eyes remain carefully blank. I was never fully successful in reading his poker face in the past but today, he seems more... cold.

Lydia looks as surprised as I feel. The contempt she flashed me with earlier through her gaze has been directed toward her son now.

"I will not tolerate incivility. Speak what you came here for and see yourself out." She tips her chin up, her diamond studs glinting through her short hair.

"Perfect." Alan drops my hand, only to wrap his arm around my shoulders. "Remember Rochelle?"

She chooses to remain silent.

"I couldn't introduce you to her the last time. Allow me to rectify my mistake. Rochelle, meet my mother. Lydia Will."

The way she refuses to meet my gaze tells me she put two and two together about what's going on between me and Alan.

"Mum, this is Rochelle Moore. My former intern, an excellent cook, and the love of my life."

Alan gazes down at me with so much love, I forget the weird feeling in my stomach.

"How old is she?" Lydia asks sternly, her eyes scanning me from head to toe.

"How is that any of your concern?" Alan cocks his head to the side.

Lydia bristles. "You don't know about the malicious intentions these young girls have, Alan. All they know is to spread their—"

A muscle jumps in his jaw. "Speak another word against her and I'll stop the checks you receive monthly."

Lydia's face reddens. "You are threatening *me*?"

"Simply stating facts. The whole point of summoning you here was to prove to Rochelle that I am done hiding her from everyone. And to warn you. Do anything to her or her family and you'll bear the consequences."

At her silence, he asks, "Are we clear?"

She jerks a nod.

He gentles his tone. "I'll always support you financially. But don't give me a reason not to."

He waits for a second, maybe expecting her to say something to salvage their relationship which was on the verge of breaking.

When she remains motionless, he takes my hand in his and bows his head in goodbye before leaving.

Alan remained silent as we rode back to the penthouse.

The heaviness in the atmosphere was palpable. He had to choose between his mother and me. The thought was eating at me throughout the drive.

Did I unintentionally create a wedge between a mother and her son? Was my demand for respect too much? With the chaos of thoughts plaguing me, I padded through the penthouse to his bedroom.

Finding the charger, I plug in my dead phone and turn it on. My phone dings with an incoming text, then another, then one more.

I frown as I try to read and make out what's happening. My eyes flit over the words and pictures.

Each message tells the same thing. I swing on my heels when I feel Alan coming from behind me.

"Ohmygod, Alan!" I cover my mouth with my hand.

"What happened?" his brows draw together, probably because of my sudden tears.

"Look," I hand him my phone.

I grin through my tears as I wrap my arms around him. "Asher proposed to Emily last night after we left."

"He did." There's a smile in his voice. His arms come around me and we stay like this for a few minutes.

"I am sorry you couldn't witness it because of me. I had my mother fly here and I wanted to show you how I didn't care about anyone else. But whatever I try to do, I end up fucking things up when it comes to you."

I pull back and shake my head adamantly. "*I* am the one who should be apologizing. Because of me, you went against your mother. I feel so bad—"

"Yes, I did it all for you. Because that's what you do when you love someone. I wanted to show you through my actions that I choose you, Rochelle. Over everything else. Only you."

My heart sings. "So, you're not mad at me?"

He chuckles. "Of course not. Are you?" he motions to the phone in his hand, indicating about missing the proposal.

"No. You know why?" I smile at him.

"Why?"

"Because I choose you too."

EPILOGUE

Five years later

Alan

"I should get going." I rise from the chair.

Mr. Taylor regards me with amusement. We were ironing out the details on the latest expansion plan of Paradise Valley.

In the last five years, our partnership has turned into a bond that I cherish in my heart.

I see him as a father figure and he adores me like a son he never had.

I now operate mainly from New York as Rochelle has her life here. I couldn't ask her to leave the country she grew up in. I didn't have anything left in London so I decided to stay here with our friends and family.

But I do have to travel once in a while as work demands.

"We still didn't cover the last point on the agenda." His eyes crinkle.

"That can wait."

The sound of his laughter echoes after me as I exit the office.

I tell the name of the restaurant to John once I am inside the car. It takes us fifteen minutes to reach there. Fifteen long minutes.

As soon as I set foot inside the restaurant, the manager rushes to me and personally shows me to a table. The one where I'll be dining with my wife. Yes, my wife.

Rochelle and I tied the knot nearly a year ago with our friends and family—except for Lydia—as our witnesses.

I wanted Rochelle to complete her education and chase her dreams before taking the big step.

There was no place for doubt when it came to Rochelle being my life partner. She was my first friend in this city who went to become my first love. And I deem myself lucky for marrying the love of my life.

I get to live with my best friend. I get to make love to her every night and dream with her.

Dream of a future filled with happiness. We got our happy ending by passing through many obstacles. I do not dare to take this life with her for granted even for a second.

Every day, like clockwise, I meet her in this restaurant.

I have rectified my past mistakes and put my wife on the top of my list of priorities.

I glance at my watch. She is ten minutes late.

The manager approaches my table with a smile, a server following him closely. I notice that the bloke is a new recruit as I have never seen him before.

"The head chef sends their regards to our regular customer in the form of the choicest of delicacies."

He claps and the server sets the plate. The manager goes on to talk about the smoked salmon with prawns but I stop him with a palm.

"As you can see, my date hasn't arrived yet." I point at the empty seat.

"You could at least have a taste. Our head chef insists."

I cock an eyebrow but comply and bring a small morsel of the food up to my lips to taste.

I don't want to eat without my wife's loving company but I have a feeling the manager wouldn't budge until he sees me taste the dish.

My eyes fall shut as I savor its flavour before swallowing.

"I'd like to have a word with this head chef of yours."

The manager pales in front of me. "Is something the matter, sir?"

Interlinking my fingers, I rest them on the table. "The head chef." I give him a look that has him stumbling to what I assume is the kitchen.

I check my phone to see if Rochelle has called. Nothing.

I frown. A shadow falls over me and I look up to find the most beautiful forest green eyes staring at me.

Dressed in a white top, and black trousers, the chef towers over my table, the emerald heart-shaped pendant glinting against her neck. Her dark locks are neatly tied up in a ponytail.

"You asked for me, sir?" The chef says.

"Yes, I did. May I ask the reason behind your generosity?" I gesture to the plate on the table.

"You were waiting for quite some time, sir and I thought as one of our regulars, we should send you a few starters while you wait." Her lips twitch.

I raise a brow. "Ah, so you feel sorry for me."

She gives a playful shrug and I stand and face her.

Grabbing her by the shoulders, I turn her around. Her arse bumps against the table.

My hand reaches up and pulls the hair tie off her ponytail.

"Alan," She breathes. And my cock hardens.

I bend and press my lips to her ear. "You are a bad, bad girl for making your husband wait like that. Are you trying to get punished, love?"

Rochelle's eyes widen. "Everyone's staring, Alan."

My wife tries to push me off her, the effort half-hearted. "So? You're the boss, you can kick everyone out right now if you want."

Rochelle shakes her head and chuckles. "*You* are the boss, husband. I am the executive cook here."

Rochelle went on to complete a thorough four-year professional culinary course.

This restaurant was a wedding gift from me which she refused to accept.

After lots of convincing, she agreed on becoming a partner and running the business as well as working as a chef here.

I tuck a strand behind her ear. "You'll have to explain the new recruit about us. That poor chap was scared shitless at the thought of offending me."

"It's your glare and that scary frown that makes everyone run the other way." She teases.

"You're not running." I tilt my head.

"Because I love you." she cups my jaw and I lean into her touch, soaking her love.

When I remain silent, she frowns. "S-say it back."

I chuckle. "I love you, Rochelle." I place a soft kiss on her forehead and she squeals.

"Ohmygod," Her beautiful greens are filled with tears as she beams at me. She grabs one of my hands and places it against her belly where our little girl is growing. "She moved."

"Say those words again." She breathes.

"I love you."

When the baby moves again, my eyes snap up to my wife.

An incredulous laugh escapes my throat. I bend to press my forehead to hers.

Moisture collects in my eyes as I watch Rochelle giggling with joy.

"I choose you," I whisper, my eyes never leaving hers as our hands come together over her swollen belly.

"I choose you, too Alan," she speaks, and just like that, I am the happiest man in the world.

The End

HEY, THERE!

Thank you so much for reading Alan and Ro's love story. This couple will always hold a special place in our hearts.

We can't believe the Sinful Series has come to an end. (Who's cutting onions?) Thank you to each and every one of you who took a chance on this debut series and showered so much love on these characters.

If you enjoyed Sinful Love, please leave a review. Spread the word around and share this book with your reader friends! It would mean a lot.

Share your thoughts here:

Amazon – www.amazon.com/author/sanjananidhi

Goodreads – www.goodreads.com/sanjananidhi

BookBub – www.bookbub.com/authors/sanjana-nidhi

ALSO BY SANJANA NIDHI

THE SINFUL SERIES

Sinful Liaisons

Sinful Lust

Sinful Love

THE RUTHLESS SERIES

My Ruthless Opponent

My Ruthless Neighbor

My Ruthless Husband

ABOUT THE AUTHORS

Sanjana and Nidhi are two sisters who share a passion for reading and writing everything romance.

They love their heroes alpha and loyal at heart.

Being hopeless romantic themselves, their books promise to have no cheating and a fulfilling HEA!

When they are not writing, the duo can be found painting and sketching or swooning over Asian dramas / Netflix shows.

Connect with Sanjana Nidhi to get the latest updates about their work and much more.

Instagram – @authorsanjananidhi

Facebook – sanjananidhi.author

Goodreads – Sanjana Nidhi

Made in the USA
Coppell, TX
27 September 2022

83678250R10225